# Other Books from Inklings

## Eclectic Writings Series Featuring Many Great Authors
Vol. 1 *Eclectically Carnal* edited by Fern Brady and Chantell Renee
Vol. 2 *Eclectically Criminal* edited by Fern Brady
Vol. 3 *Eclectically Vegas, Baby!* edited by Fern Brady
Vol. 4 *Eclectically Cosmic* edited by Fern Brady

## Books by Inklings Author, Ramon Del Villar
*Payback*, Book 1 in the Roberto Duran Series
*An Interpreters Anatomy of A Civil Lawsuit*, in English and Spanish

## Books by Inklings Author, Meg Hafdahl
*Twisted Reveries: Thirteen Tales of the Macabre*
*Twisted Reveries 2: Tales from Willoughby*

## Books by Inklings Author, Melissa Algood
*Blood on the Potomac*

## From Inklings International
*Florilegio Poético* del poeta Flavio Hinojosa, Jr.

## From Inklings Children Division
*The Smiley Face Blatoon* by Lady Nefari Ydarb
Vol. 1 *Perceptions: Special Needs* edited by Fern Brady

# Eclectically Vegas, Baby!

## Eclectic Writings Series Vol. 3

Edited by

## Fern Brady

Inklings
Publishing

www.inklingspublishing.com

*Eclectically Vegas, Baby!: Eclectic Writings Series Vol. 3*

Edited by Fern Brady
Copyedited/Formatted
by D Tinker
Cover Art by Verstandt

ISBN: 978-0-99102-119-2 by Inklings Publishing
http://inklingspublishing.com

First US Edition
Printed in the United States of America
21  20  19  18  17        2  3  4  5

*To Mike Brady*

*Thank you for always being
there for me.
Thank you for all your
love and support.*

# CONTENTS

# ACKNOWLEDGMENTS

Inklings Publishing is pleased to bring to you volume three of the Eclectic Writings Series. When we put out the call for submissions for Vegas stories, we expected to receive some very run-of-the-mill accounts of Vegas doings. We were pleasantly surprised when these wonderfully eclectic tales came in. Each, in their own way, does homage to our series' pledge to bring unexpected twists and unusual stories to readers.

The most important gratitude is, as always, to God, whose grace and favor have built Inklings Publishing up. His guidance, love, and mercy keep Inklings going through tough times and bring us new connections to take this small press to new levels. May we always remember to walk in His ways. May His leadership be our very present help and source of direction.

Fern Brady sends out a word of gratitude to her awesome husband, Mike Brady, for supporting her and giving her dreams the chance to take flight. Thanks also goes to her wonderful family, who worry about her, encourage her, and have ever been her biggest fans.

The Inklings canine family suffered the loss of Ella this year, and she will be forever in our hearts. To Coco, Arwen, Merlin, and Grace go lots of hugs and kisses for brightening every day with their cuteness and loyalty.

To the Houston Writers Guild family, a special thank you for letting Inklings help you sell your books as a bookseller and for giving us new venues through which to bring our books to new fans.

To our readership, thank you for purchasing our books and supporting small businesses. We look forward to helping create new jobs and bringing new voices to our world!

# TIME

*ANDREA BARBOSA*

Vegas seemed an unlikely place for a dying person. Such an agitated, frenzied, furious city didn't appear to be an adequate destination. A person's last days should be spent resting, forgiving, and pondering what was left undone, unsaid, and unfinished—in peace.

That's not what she wanted, though. She didn't want to revisit feelings that would have no meaning soon. She didn't want resentment to consume her final days with excuses for what she'd never done—she needed to use this elusive time to make memories.

"How on earth are we going to travel around the world? You're in no physical condition to endure a trip! Besides, that would cost us a fortune! Around the world? You just—I don't think we can!"

Her husband's response to her last wish had not surprised her. What was the excuse this time? No money? No time? No health?

"Is it always about money?" Her eyes focused on him from across the bedroom where she sat in the rocking chair by the window. Money—stupid paper, preventing dreams from coming true. There was never enough of it to do what mattered most in life—to live and be happy. So much was left undone because of it.

"Money? Well, no . . . it's about . . . you, of course. You just—I don't think you can. You shouldn't. It will take a toll on you. You won't withstand the long haul." He stood by the door, afraid to come inside the room. Her intimidating stare warned him not to get close. She knew that the loss would be too much for him to bear, but would he regret the time he didn't spend with her? Where did their quality time go? It was about money, indeed. His job had been to provide shelter, food . . . and quality of life. Or was it quantity of life?

"It is about me. You're right. And I want to do this. I will do this. A pretend around-the-world trip."

" 'A pretend around-the-world trip'? What do you mean?" he asked, looking confused.

"Take a guess. There is one place on the planet where we can 'visit' Paris, Egypt, New York, Venice, Monte Carlo . . . let me see, where else? Oh, yes! There's Rome, Tuscany, and New Orleans, as well! And we can do it in one weekend. I'm sure I can handle a weekend 'around the world.' " She chuckled.

"Las Vegas? Are you talking about Vegas? Your last wish is to gamble?" her husband asked in disbelief. Guilt mingled with a hint of relief on his face.

She wondered if the guilty feeling would creep up on him like a dark shadow in an alley. Would knowing he had never taken her on a proper vacation feel like the sour taste of a bad hangover? Was the cruel realization that she was now too sick to travel too shocking for him to accept? Would it haunt him forever if she died without having seen the world? He would have to agree to her last wish before it was too late. Wasn't there enough money now? It was not an ideal trip—and by no means the best situation or scenario. She could gamble and even afford to lose some. She was dying, after all. Her fragile body's weakened limbs might not survive a plane ride, and the thrill of a vacation might be too much for her feeble heart to endure. But it was the least she expected him to do for her.

"Yes, Bill, Vegas. Vegas! Get it? But not to gamble. No, no, no gambling; that's the last thing I'm looking forward to. Look at it in a special way. The hotels and casinos all have different themes and are like mini-cities or mini-countries. We can embrace Vegas like a version of Disney's It's a Small World. Not to gamble, do you understand? So, what do you think?" The sarcasm in her voice was gone. She sounded energized, emitting a peaceful aura around her as if there was nothing wrong with going on a trip, as if she still had her whole life ahead of her.

"Yes, I guess . . . a small world of sorts. . . . Are you sure you can handle it? Kelly, sweetie, I want to make sure you're well if you are to endure this extravagant deed. We will talk to Dr. Ravi tomorrow and see what he says about it."

"Bill, I want to go to Las Vegas, regardless of what Dr. Ravi says. Even if he doesn't agree with it, I know I can. It's my last wish, and I will do it. I won't die without seeing the world, even if it's the artificial world of Vegas."

"Las Vegas . . . I don't know. . . . "

"I've been planning it out. There's so much to do there! We'll stay at The Venetian. I've always dreamed about going to Venice. It's so romantic! They even have gondolas, like the real Venice."

"Gondolas?"

"Yes, gondolas. Then, we will go to Paris and climb the Eiffel Tower. Another completely romantic setting! And we can visit the pyramids, dressed like archeologists. Caesars Palace will be great for Rome. Oh, I can just dream of all these places! There's more to Vegas than gambling!" She stood up from the chair and turned her back to him, looking out the window and dreaming of a world beyond her reach. Suddenly, she turned around to face him. "Remember the movie?"

"Movie? What movie?" His eyes moved around, searching for the answer somewhere.

Shame on him for never remembering things she liked. He was always working, taking the little things for granted. She wished he had enjoyed going to the movies with her. He was always busy, trying to make ends meet, trying to earn more, and for what? No time for silly entertainment.

"*Blade Runner!*" she said with a hint of impatience. "The last scene. The replicant's last words. Remember?"

His expression didn't show any signs that he recalled the last scene she was talking about. His face looked as if he saw only empty space inside his mind, trying to bring forth a memory he didn't have.

" 'I've . . . seen things you people wouldn't believe. . . . ' " she started. Bill shook his head again in resignation and left the room in silence.

"He definitely doesn't remember," she whispered to herself, rolling her eyes in annoyance. *The only problem,* she thought, *is that I haven't seen anything and my time is almost up.*

-$-

The next day, Bill took her for her weekly checkup. After the nurse checked her vital signs, she led them to the examination room. By now, Kelly could navigate the hospital almost as well as she did her home. She knew nearly every nurse, fellow, and doctor around. She had been struggling with this terrible disease for over four years. The tests, treatment, office visits, consultations—they were all as integral a part of her routine as her daily shower. The most unlikely place for her to feel comfortable—a hospital.

After they'd waited for about ten minutes, Dr. Ravi came into the room, inspecting the chart the nurse had left hanging by the door.

"How are you feeling today, Kelly? Your vital signs are looking good!"

"I'm feeling great, Dr. Ravi. I haven't felt like this in a while. I have a renewed boost of energy, and I feel as if I can travel around the world!"

Dr. Ravi smiled and came closer to her, placing his stethoscope on her chest. "Take a deep breath for me," he said. "What happened for you to be so happy? Are you not in pain?"

She breathed in and out, and he moved the stethoscope to her back, asking her to breathe deeply again. "I'm going on a trip around the world," she said after exhaling.

Dr. Ravi stopped the examination and faced her, frowning. "A trip around the world, you say?"

"She's joking, Dr. Ravi," Bill said quickly before Kelly could respond, and she sensed the embarrassment in her husband's voice.

"I'm glad you are joking," Dr. Ravi answered. "You are in no shape to travel, Kelly. I'm sorry to tell you that."

"Dr. Ravi, I'm not taking a real trip around the world. We're going to Vegas," she said.

"If you say she can, Dr. Ravi. I don't want her to do anything to deteriorate her condition," Bill intervened. She rolled her eyes at him.

Dr. Ravi sat on the nearby stool, looking at both of them for a few minutes. Kelly knew he was pondering the best way to let her know she couldn't materialize her dreams.

"Kelly," he started in the gentlest voice possible. "You know your condition is getting worse. There's no cure. The clinical trial is not working as effectively as we had predicted. There has been no significant improvement, and there has been no stabilization either. The tumor is still spreading, and you're in a very delicate situation. Leaving town is not a good idea. You need to stay close to the hospital. Taking a trip is not advisable. You would be very tired. You would need to carry portable oxygen, and you're on a lot of medication. A lot of things could go wrong. I really don't think you should go anywhere."

Kelly's expression didn't change. She was motivated by her desire and determination to take her Vegas "tour of the world." Time was not on her side.

"See, baby. Dr. Ravi doesn't recommend this trip. Let's just go home, and I'll buy a couple of videos of the places you want to go, and we can watch them and pretend we're there. Isn't that a great idea?" Bill asked, fidgeting with his car keys, visibly nervous as he sensed Kelly wasn't about to give up.

"I know my body by now. And I know what I can handle. I can do this. I know I can. I have nothing to lose. I'm going to die sooner or later. The treatment is not working, and I'm well aware of that, Dr. Ravi. I've always wanted to see the world. The least I can do before I die is pretend to see the world, but not just on a TV screen. In a fake reality, true—but I need to feel it. I need to be somewhere. I need to see it, need to walk through it. And I've already decided."

Dr. Ravi shook his head. "Kelly, you're very weak now. If you accidentally fall and break a bone, or cut yourself and get an infection, there could be complications, which wouldn't be easy to deal with. You need to take these things into consideration."

Bill looked at Kelly with a hint of hope, but there was no way Dr. Ravi could talk sense into her stubborn mind. She was determined.

"I'm well aware, Dr. Ravi; I am. And thank you for pointing out all that could go wrong with me. But this is the last chance I have before I'm admitted into palliative care, or before I'm unable to walk or move. I'm willing to accept the risks and take this chance. My time's up."

"I can't forbid you to do what you want, Kelly. I can simply suggest and advise. I don't recommend you take such an unsafe trip. If there's anything I can say to change your mind . . . "

"No, Dr. Ravi, there's nothing you can say to change my mind" was her resolute response.

"Well . . . then . . . Bill, make sure to keep an eye on her. And call me if anything happens. I know a doctor in Vegas and can give you his number in case you need local assistance. Kelly, please. Don't force yourself to do anything bold. No strenuous activities. And make sure to take all your medication at their scheduled times. I will see you again next week."

"Thanks, Dr. Ravi. Everything will work out fine. I'll bring you a souvenir," Kelly said.

-$-

They left the hospital in silence. Kelly was adamant about the trip. Nothing was going to change her mind. Bill walked next to her with his head down. In contrast, she was smiling, uncaring of the consequences of taking such a risky trip, and she exuded such joy that one might think she had received news that she was cured.

"Don't be so reluctant," Kelly said when Bill opened the car door for her to get inside. He closed the door after she buckled the seat belt, and walked around to take his place in the driver's seat.

"The doctor should have insisted that you not go," he said, shaking his head.

"Bill, let me tell you something. Even if Dr. Ravi had forbidden me to, I'd still go. The only way for him or you to stop me is to hospitalize me. Period. Forget about it, and please, let's try to have a good time. Forget I'm dying. Everyone's dying, all right? Once you're born, you're condemned to death. Think about it. Everyone's time is limited."

"Everyone will die eventually, of course, Kelly dear, but we don't know when! In your case, your days are numbered. And I don't want any chances of speeding that up and cutting short my time with you even more."

"Bill, you have had all the time in the world with me, haven't you? But you've never bothered to make the best of it. It's only when there's no more time that you've realized what you will be missing. I wish you would have realized it sooner."

Bill reached for her hand and squeezed it tight. Kelly knew the thought of losing her was surreal to him. He had told her he had no idea what he was going to do without her. Maybe her words had been too harsh, but she knew she was speaking a truth she couldn't hold inside any longer. Although they had been married for twenty years, there had been no children. Apparently it was his fault—some affliction the doctor had told them about long ago but which she couldn't remember now. They had tried in vitro fertilization, but it hadn't worked. After a few failed attempts and two miscarriages, they gave up. They had thought about adopting, but it never really came about.

Always the money issue. *Maybe later, when there's more money . . . maybe in a few years*—it was the excuse she always heard. Kelly knew Bill had to reconsider her request. It would be their only trip, and it had to be memorable. For her, for him . . . for them. For time. Was there any chance for redemption now? No. There was no more time left. Las Vegas would save time, but it would also steal time. It would save her the time that a trip around the world might take, but it would steal her time if she couldn't handle the adventure.

-$-

Death had taken a different meaning since Kelly accepted that it was imminent. She hated to be so close to it, but at the same time, it gave her an unusual perspective. Although she didn't want to harbor any hard feelings toward her husband of twenty years, she resented him. All the missed opportunities! Why hadn't she left him long ago? What did Bill do for her, after all? Yes, he was a "good" husband. He worked hard and paid the bills; he was a faithful man, always next to her. He cared about her. He didn't want anything bad to happen to her.

But it was not enough. He never took an interest in her hobbies or took her out to dance, to travel, to the movies—or even just to enjoy life. He was always immersed in his work, always tired, always bored.

Had he always been like this? She couldn't remember back to when she fell in love with him. It was a long time ago. While Life was happening, Bill had always seemed to be waiting for a better moment, for more money, for another opportunity, or for something else that never came. Kelly was about to embrace Death. Would Death remember what her favorite movie was? Would Death take her on a vacation around the world? By then, Bill would be alone. Bill would have to face Life. And Life would not be as gentle as Death. Life would certainly nudge him on a daily basis and not let him forget. Life was unrelenting. Death was forgiving. Her dream could make her forgive. Her dream could be the redeeming answer before she embraced the journey to her final destination.

-$-

Her body was shutting down—little by little, breath by breath, organ by organ. She couldn't tell which one was stopping first, but she knew it was time to go. The image that came to mind, as it always did when she thought about the end, was of Rutger Hauer's character in *Blade Runner*.

"All those . . . moments will be lost . . . in time . . . like . . . tears . . . in rain," the replicant had said before his system shut down.

Was it time to say goodbye and sleep forever? What would she lose in the rain? Time? All those moments that never were? Close to the end, when time became a rare commodity, it became relevant. But despite its presumed significance, it carried no relevance. Like tears in rain; like time in space.

The fragile, beaten-up body, the box that contained her soul, had served its purpose. There were no signs of pain, no signs of discomfort, and no signs of distress. Time to say goodbye to the world. Time for a new destination. Time to die. Time.

# ROLLING THE DICE IN SIN CITY
*CAROLINE SPOSTO*

It was damned dark in the Mojave Desert after midnight. We could look up at the vast onyx sky and see it awash with thousands of stars. It made us want to make love, but the interior of Jim's Honda Civic was too small and the hood of his car was too hot. Parched winds made chaos of our hair and reddened our eyes. I stumbled over the rocky soil in my six-inch stiletto pumps. Jim found my arm in the blackness. We kissed, laughed, and got hot and heavy.

Half an hour later, we shambled back into the car like children with a secret. We were windblown, rumpled, and looking at another hour on I-15. We cranked up the Stray Cats. We even finished the cokes, melted ice and all, from our last stop—Barstow Station's McDonald's, the retrofitted train car in the then-tiny town that is the halfway mark between LA and Vegas.

It was 1991, and we were in our midtwenties, eloping without fanfare. Both products of suburbia but doing our best to be badass bohemians, we shared a lot of chemistry and a truth-or-dare dynamic.

-$-

Eleven months earlier, on our second date, we leased a Hollywood apartment and moved in together. Despite our outward recklessness and cavalier talk, we were never really okay with our cohabitation. Still, we hosted a guilt-ridden-and-living-in-sin housewarming party to introduce our friends to each other. On the way home from target practice at the pistol range, Jim bought a funky diamond-chip ring for the fourth finger of my left hand with his pocket money.

Beneath our in-your-face bravado, we were go-to-work-every-day good citizens having a bit of flamboyant fun. We never thought about five minutes into the future, let alone years. Life was good . . . until our well-intentioned friends—Jim's mostly—paved the proverbial road to hell in our honor.

We were invited to a dinner party: great food, plenty of wine, all our favorite people. By the end of the evening, the candles had burned low and their flames danced on shiny pools of wax. The tablecloth was littered with dessert crumbs, and the conversation rambled with delightful spontaneity over our second cups of coffee. We barely noticed our host disappear into his kitchen with a couple other guests until they burst back into the room with a well-rehearsed "surprise" speech that came with the presentation of a few gag gifts.

It wasn't a dinner party; it was an engagement party. A surprise engagement party! *Our* surprise engagement party! I choked on my coffee and strained my peripheral vision in Jim's direction to see if he too was in an agony of thinly disguised terror.

He was, of course, because we weren't engaged.

Damned sobering. Almost sickening. But they had gone to so much trouble, had spent so much money, and were so pleased with themselves that neither Jim nor I had the heart to spoil the evening.

We both played along, figuring it would all blow over. It would have too, but word of the party got back to Jim's mother, who phoned us a few days later, all excited, to ask when the wedding would be. The date? I doubt we even owned a calendar.

We dodged the question, and for the first few weeks it was an intermittent drip, like Chinese water torture. It worked our nerves, but we could take it. Then Jim's aunts joined in, and it crescendoed, full blast, like one of those fire hoses used to break up civil unrest in the 1960s.

Jim was an aspiring filmmaker who paid his half of the rent peddling cheap off-brand boom boxes and novelty items. I was a struggling actress who worked part time teaching English to refugees, filled in for movie studio secretaries on Jewish holidays, and assisted a wedding disc jockey on weekends.

Jim's parents were traditional, conservative, stable, and uptight. Mine lived in Colorado, were divorced, and at that period of their lives, couldn't stand each other. Although I often talked to my father on the phone, I hadn't seen him in a couple years and didn't even have his address. He was tired and struggling to fight his way back from a financial reversal. My mother had her own problems. Even if we had been planning on a wedding—*which we weren't*—I didn't want them to fly to LA, and I couldn't ask them for money.

And yet, for reasons I still can't articulate, the matrimony machine kept coming toward us like a steamroller about to squash a pair of Hostess Twinkies. More and more, our stroll-in-the-park lifestyle felt like a one-way trek across the Bridge of Sighs.

Three or so months into this insanity, we ended up at an evening wedding reception of a couple long since messily divorced. It was quite the posh suburban '90s soiree, if you know what I mean.

I sat at the table making mental calculations of the cost of the hall, the pink bridesmaids' dresses, the chalky pillow mints, the centerpieces with flocked doves and plastic bells, the chicken cutlets, the big cake with gooey scarlet roses, the pink napkins and pleated linens . . .

*Is this what we're supposed to do? Shit!*

When it got to five figures, I almost threw up.

"Jim," I whispered, leaning in close to him. "Let's just go to Vegas and get it over with."

He paused for a moment, surveying the scene. "No shit," he said.

We left quickly and quietly, hopping into the Civic at twilight's last gleam to speed east on I-15, singing along with Oingo Boingo at the top of our lungs.

-$-

This was pre-Trump Vegas—a tawdrier place devoid of even the slightest premonition of the sanitized postmodern replicas of the world's wonders that define it now. It was an era before white-bread Midwestern tax accountants went to conventions with spouses in tow, amicably parroting and paraphrasing the line "What happens in Vegas stays in Vegas."

We drove through the shorter version of the Strip, while billboards beckoned us with buffets and lighted marquees dazzled us with names of entertainers. This was pre-GPS, so we wandered around, went on a hunch, followed signs, and ended up asking a cop, but eventually we found city hall.

After one in the morning, beneath the greenish fluorescent lights in a work-worn government building, everything looks preternaturally crummy. Not just the objects but the people too: the civil servants and all the couples in line—*especially us*.

I don't remember what paperwork we needed. In those days, we all carried our social security cards around in our wallets. Maybe we stopped and picked up our birth certificates on the way. That and a couple of crumpled twenties got us a marriage license.

*Helluva lot easier than a driver's license. Helluva lot faster than a dog license. Helluva shelf life, 'til death do us part.*

A marriage license doesn't count until someone official utters an incantation, sort of like when Tinker Bell came back to life after the children clapped their hands and said they believed. Those magic words were the final item on the list for our scavenger hunt.

"We're off to see the wizard, baby," Jim said, sounding a little shaky.

"You can still back out," I said, as much to myself as to him.

He shook his head.

We drove down Las Vegas Boulevard South, a stretch festooned with too-cute Disneyland-scale chapels. Trouble was, most of them were closed. It was going on two in the morning. I spotted a fat man in a polyester suit smoking a cigarette in the doorway of a little white building with a steeple. He reminded me of the comedian Louie Anderson, so I assumed he'd be pleasant.

"Let's see if he can marry us," I said.

Jim made a bank robber–style U-turn, jolted the car to a stop, and ran around to open my door. We trotted up the sidewalk.

"What can I do for you?" the fat man asked without smiling.

Since we were a young couple and this was a wedding chapel, it seemed like a strange question. But then, it was late, even by Vegas standards, and Jim and I looked more bedraggled than freshly rolled drunks.

"We're here to get married," Jim informed him.

The fat man threw his cigarette into the bushes and ushered us inside. He then picked up the receiver of an old black push-button phone, dialed a number, waited a moment, and then put it down. "Paging the reverend," he said.

Jim paid while I went to the ladies' room to freshen up. Someone had left an Ace pocket comb on the counter. It looked clean, but I washed it anyway before attacking the snarls that tangled my hair like Gordian knots.

I came back to find Jim going through a wedding menu that was loaded with à la carte options.

"Flowers?" the fat man asked, pointing at a bouquet that looked even more tired than we were. We shook our heads.

"Video?" he suggested.

We laughed. "No, thanks."

"Rings?"

We looked at each other, knowing we had only a couple hundred bucks between us and still needed a room for the night.

"Do you have any really *cheap* rings?" I asked.

He gave Jim a deadpan look, reached under the counter, and took out a case of bubblegum-machine-quality pot metal rings.

"Thirty-five bucks," he said.

It was a rip-off, but we bought them anyway. We also went for the Polaroid pictures.

"I'll even throw in music," he told us in the tone of voice one might use when giving away a million dollars. He excavated a beat-up cassette tape from a cluttered drawer.

The entrance bell chimed, marking Reverend Cotton's entrance. He was a well-dressed sixty-something African American Pentecostal minister. His impenetrable poker face made me wonder if he had been giving last rites or bending his elbow in a local bar when he got the fat man's page. But once he introduced himself, his chess-bishop face broke into a broad, gleaming smile. He congratulated Jim and gave us each a strong, warm handshake. We liked him very much right away.

A brief, breathless silence filled the room.

*It was time.*

"You go up to the altar," the fat man told Jim. "And *you*," he said, meaning me, "stay here. Then, when I start the music, walk slowly down the aisle."

I waved my hands at the empty chapel, protesting. "Nobody's here but us. Can't I just start at the altar too? I mean, it seems sort of . . ."

"No!" he snapped. "That's not how you do a wedding! You stay here, and when I start the music, you walk!"

"Right," I said, too worn out to fight with him.

He pressed a button on the cassette player, Wagner's wedding march started, and I walked down the aisle between the empty seats in time with the music. The chapel wasn't very big, but it seemed to take forever.

The chapel phone rang.

"Hang on!" the fat man shouted, cutting off the music. I froze in my tracks, three-quarters of the way there.

The fat man started yelling into the phone. "Yeah. I know what goddamned time it is! Where the hell do you think I am? Huh? What the hell else would I be doing? I'm doing a goddamned wedding, that's what the hell I'm doing!" He slammed the receiver and looked at me. "Come back here, miss," he said. "We'll have to do it again."

Before I could protest, he rewound the cassette with a squeal. Jim stood at the altar with a useless groom-in-the-headlights look on his face. I was on my own.

Knowing it was a lost cause, I went back to square one. This time we got from the first beat of the march to "You may kiss the bride" without incident. Then we signed the marriage license.

*Side note: Marriage licenses are full of invisible ink that doesn't show up for a while: clauses about cooking, cleaning, sex, money, and family. Anyone who has signed one knows what I mean.*

On our way to the car, I looked into Jim's eyes and whispered, "My feet are killing me."

"We should have brought a change of clothes," he said.

We found an all-night gift shop and bought cheap flip-flops, I heart Vegas T-shirts, and baggy Hawaiian-print pants. Then we drove out past the dazzling part of the Strip to find a cheap motel.

By the time we got to our room, the sun was coming up. My worn-out groom carried me across the threshold, dropping me on the bed like a duffel bag. We slept.

The next day, we woke up late and devoured a starch-and-grease all-you-can-eat breakfast buffet that included Tang instead of orange juice. I got a fistful of quarters for the payphone and called my father. "Daddy, I got married last night," I announced.

"To who?" he replied.

*I don't recall the rest of the conversation.*

Then, I called my DJ boss and explained why I wouldn't be at that afternoon's gig. He congratulated me and then fired me.

*Should've put the damned quarters into the slot machines.*

On the way home, we toured Hoover Dam. Jim marveled at the engineering while I got depressed about the construction workers who died due to the high wire act it had taken to build it.

When we returned to Los Angeles, Jim's father greeted him with "Is she pregnant?" (I was not.)

-$-

The marriage lasted twenty-three years. During that time we built a small business and raised two daughters, who are now grown. Then one day, as spontaneously as he had suggested the apartment and as boldly as he had proposed, Jim asked to be unmarried.

I didn't see the end coming, and it wasn't my idea. The homewrecker I imagined waiting in the wings, whose existence Jim denied, never stepped into the spotlight. Either she got cold feet or he was telling the truth all along. My rebel husband refused counseling, so that was that. Our wild ride was over, and I doubt premarital counseling, matching bridesmaids, or pillow mints would have changed a damned thing.

What we imagine is seldom what we actually get. Though Jim isn't in the picture anymore, I still have a faded Vegas chapel Polaroid as a souvenir of that flawed engagement and absurd wedding. On good days, it reminds me to laugh at myself, trust my instincts, and not expect perfection. After all, as my father used to say, *life is just an adventure!*

Romantics are called hopeless for a reason. I know it all too well. It wouldn't surprise me if someday, even at fifty-three or ninety-three, I once again found myself in the Las Vegas courthouse on the arm of a handsome man. No doubt we'd apply for a marriage license at midnight with the same passion, optimism, and bravado of my first foray to Vegas!

# SUN DAY

*DANIEL O'CONNOR*

It was too bright and cheery a day for the world to end.

That was what ran through his mind as he ended the phone call. He had come to Las Vegas for a few days of stress relief with his best friend, Shariq. That friend was last seen passed out on, or near, his bed in their suite on the eighth floor. Dempsey had been lounging by the pool at the Golden Nugget Hotel and Casino for the past hour.

Two days earlier, after unpacking his clothes from his luggage, he had convinced himself that he'd filled that same suitcase with all of his troubles and zipped it closed, not to be opened until he was ready to return to the real world.

Tucked inside his Samsonite, he'd stashed away his divorce, his quest to find his seven-year-old daughter and begin the healing process, his stock market losses, his chronic back pain, and his lack of advancement at work.

Now poolside, his phone still in hand, he scanned his surroundings. The sun was bright, not a cloud to be seen in the blue desert sky. People frolicked in the clear swimming pool. Children of all ages blasted through the transparent, fully-enclosed three-story water slide, which took them zipping through an enormous tank filled with live sharks. It was completely safe, but a little scary nonetheless. Dempsey so wanted to try it, but his lifelong battle with aquaphobia prevented it. He was probably more fearful of the swimming pool, even one in which he could stand, than he was of the sharks.

Then there were the women—beautiful, bikini-clad party girls who had left their inhibitions back in Kansas, or wherever the hell they were from. Some jiggled to the poolside rock music being piped in from God knew where. Dempsey had struck out with a couple of them already, blaming his pale skin and farmer's tan, but he had vowed that he wasn't going to pay for sex.

When he'd awoken that morning, he had thought today, Cinco de Mayo, would be the charmed one. He'd win some money at the blackjack tables and score at least one pretty young companion for the evening.

That was all before the phone call.

Now he knew there would be none of that. He had only minutes to live. So did they. So did everyone.

The hypnotic, Middle East–inspired pounding of the classic Led Zeppelin song "Kashmir" started. A couple of sun worshippers let out hoots of approval.

Dempsey loved the song but knew it was rather long. He'd be dead before it ended.

He downed the rest of his beer and rifled through the little black mesh tote bag he'd brought poolside with him. He picked through towels, magazines, and various belongings until he found his prescription bottle. On days when his lower back caused him too much discomfort, he would take out a white Percocet tablet, break it in half, and down it. His recommended dosage was four pills a day, but he never took more than half a pill. He didn't want to become dependent, so he suffered through the more than thirty minutes it took to get any relief.

This time, he dropped seven or eight whole pills on the glass tabletop and ground them down to a powder with the bottom of his Bud Light bottle. On top of his pool bag was a small laminated card. It had been handed to him on the Strip. It featured a beautiful blonde who, the card suggested, would come to your room if you called the number on the back. Dempsey knew that the woman who would actually be at his door would more than likely look like the female who handed him the card: oval in shape, with the head of a box turtle.

22

"Oh, let the sun beat down upon my face, and stars fill my dream," sang Robert Plant, as the Led Zeppelin song filled the dry desert air.

He rolled up the whore card and snorted his powdered pills.

"Whoa, honey! You can't be doing that stuff. They'll toss you on the street."

He lifted his face, dusted off the tip of his nose, and looked at the pool waitress. Despite his transgression, she was smiling.

"The Golden Nugget don't stand for drug use on the property. There's families here. How 'bout you settle for another beer? I'll bring you a shot, too."

She may have been the most startling woman he'd seen in Vegas yet. His mind, though racing, gave him this initial thought: *She could've been in Destiny's Child.*

She was slim, tall, and dark, with the brightest smile. She was looking into his eyes, not searching for his wallet or trying to size up his potential wealth from a wristwatch or pricey sunglasses.

She was carrying an empty tray, ready to take his next drink order.

"It's fine. I'm sorry," he replied. All he could think about was that this sweet, lovely girl was spending her final breaths waiting on others.

"Don't look so down," she said. "You're in Vegas!"

"You should put that tray down and just sit with me here."

"Well, you don't waste any time," she laughed. "You seem nice and all," she continued, before leaning in and whispering, "despite the whole, you know, snorting shit up your nose pastime."

"That's not something—"

"One, I'm working, sweetheart, and two, I've got a big, crazy husband and a little boy, so all I can offer you is a smile and a drink."

"You have a child?"

"Sure do. Took me a long time to fit back into this outfit, too. Nothin' comes easy."

"Where is your boy right now?"

"He's at home with my mama. She takes care of him during the day. Why would you be so interested in that, Mr. . . . ?"

"Dempsey."

"Nice to meet you, Mr. Dempsey."

"No 'mister'; just Dempsey."

"Dempsey, my name is Kalela. How 'bout that beer?"

"I'd love for you to sit down here and call your son on the phone. Do you have a photo of him?"

"I've met some weird ones, but this is a first."

"No, really. Please. Let me show you my daughter."

He went back into the bag and found his wallet. He took a bent photo from it.

"You don't keep your pictures on your phone?"

"Not her pictures."

He placed the photograph on the table, securing it from the breeze's grasp by putting the empty beer bottle atop one of the bent corners. Grains of pulverized Percocet migrated from the bottom of the bottle onto the snapshot.

"This is Dana," he said.

Kalela leaned over.

"Aww, so pretty," she said.

"I haven't seen or spoken to her for almost a year."

"What?"

"My ex-wife has her. I'm not entirely sure where, and I don't even have a phone number. It's in the courts, but . . . "

"It'll all work out, Dempsey."

"Please sit down with me, Kala."

"It's Ka-le-la, and I can't sit down. My boss will have my ass."

"Look," he said, once again digging into his wallet, "I will give you all I have on me as a tip—it's probably five hundred dollars—if you'll just sit here and call your son. You can use my phone. But you need to do it quickly."

"For real?"

"Yes. Just tell him you love him and you'll always love him."

"I don't know. . . . "

"It's your job to please your guests. I'll explain it to your boss if it comes to that. The money is yours. Please, Kalela."

He could see her thinking it over as the Led Zeppelin song droned on. "All I see turns to brown," came the distant and hypnotic voice from the speakers, "as the sun burns the ground."

She sat down beside Dempsey, resting her drink tray on the table right beside the photo of his little girl. She put her hand out, palm facing up. He placed the stack of cash in it and closed her grip. It felt nice to touch her skin.

"My hand was reachin' out for the phone, but this'll work too."

He smiled and handed her the cell phone. He was beginning to feel the effects of his big snort, and his heart rate seemed to slow a bit. She began to press the screen.

"This better not be some trick for you to save my number and pester my ass," she mumbled.

"Not at all," he said. "I promise."

"Five big bills just to call my little William. That's the deal of the century."

"William," whispered Dempsey to himself, as if he'd never heard the name before. He was staring down at Dana's photo when a big hand touched his shoulder.

"Good afternoon, sir. I need to ask you to come with us, please."

There were three men in nicely pressed suits that were surely too heavy for this hot Vegas weather.

"My name is Thomas," said the burly fellow with his hand on Dempsey. "We'll need to chat with you about some of your poolside activities today, and we'll need to do it inside, in our office, please."

Before Dempsey could respond, Kalela sprung to her feet.

"Sorry, Mr. Pirics," she said to Thomas. "This gentleman asked me to sit because—"

"Not now, Kalela," he responded. "You'll be speaking to your shift manager about that. We need to escort this fellow away from the other guests for the time being."

Kalela put the phone down on the table just as the men "assisted" Dempsey to his feet. As they brought him up, one of them knocked into the table, tipping the beer bottle over and freeing the photo of little Dana to ride off on the breeze.

"My picture!" yelled Dempsey.

He watched it briefly touch the ground, just beside a woman lathering on some tanning lotion, before it took flight again and found its way into the swimming pool.

"Come with us, sir. We'll do our best to retrieve your photograph. It will probably wind up in the filter system."

They picked up his bag and took his phone from the table.

"Let Kalela have the phone, please," he pleaded.

They ignored him as they firmly led him away. He turned back to her.

"Find another phone. Call your boy now, please. Right now. A deal's a deal."

As he was being pulled away, his head remained turned toward her. She still stared at him. Their eyes locked. He watched her turn toward the pool—and the photo.

As they got him inside the hotel, he noticed that the prevailing scent was no longer chlorine but the enticing aromas of an Italian restaurant. He stopped walking.

"Sir, we don't want to have to drag you," Thomas said.

"Just hear me out for one second," Dempsey said. "I don't want to say this too loudly, but I really need to get that photo of my daughter and I desperately want to hear Kalela tell her son that she loves him. Please."

"We have to go to the office. Then we can talk about all that."

"There's no time for that," answered Dempsey. The blast of crushed Percocet made him feel as if he was watching this exchange as a third party. He felt as if he were outside of his own body.

"I don't want to cause panic," he continued. "But you all are grown men and professionals, so I will tell you right now. If there is someone you love, you have just moments to call them and tell them how you feel. Don't say why. Don't alarm them, but do it."

"What are you rambling about?"

He brought his voice to a barely audible whisper. "The world, and life as we know it, is about to end. I mean within minutes. Surely less than four or five minutes. I just want Kalela to call her son, and I want that picture of my daughter. That's it."

"What the hell did you snort?"

"No. That was just to calm myself. I'm terrified."

"You can sleep it off in the office."

They began to tug on him more forcefully, but he knew they'd go to great extremes in order to avoid a scene in front of hotel guests. Force was always a last resort.

"I don't want to hit you with this all at once," said Dempsey. "But you leave me no choice."

They stopped again. Dempsey figured that Thomas might just let him speak his piece in order to smoothly and quietly transport him to the office once he'd concluded.

"Okay, let's hear it. Keep it short, and for God's sake, keep it hushed."

The two security men with Thomas looked at each other with sighs and eye rolls.

Dempsey's whisper was a bit slurred now. "The sun is going to consume the earth," he said. "We won't feel a thing, but we're all going to evaporate." He was spewing words like lightning now. "I know it sounds crazy, but it's true," he said.

"What a crackpot," mumbled one of the officers.

"No. Look in my wallet," he said. "Go ahead."

"All right. Do it," said Thomas, hoping to calm the situation.

The other officer fumbled through the cashless wallet.

"There. My ID card," said Dempsey.

The guard pulled it out. Thomas didn't focus on the photo at first, or the small print. He just saw the big white letters in the blue circle: NASA.

Dempsey could see the muscles around Thomas's mouth moving, tightening. His eyes did not blink. His Adam's apple jumped. Then, he cleared his throat.

"So, you're some NASA bigwig, eh? You an astronaut?"

The guards snickered.

"I'm not an astronaut or a bigwig. I do work for NASA and have for twelve years."

"What do you take us for?" asked Thomas. "Are we supposed to believe that you knew the world was going to end in, er, minutes, so you decided to try and pick up a cocktail waitress at the Golden Nugget? Getting a hooker is much faster and a sure thing, Buck Rogers."

"No. I do work for NASA, but my clearance is low. I don't know what we're working on most of the time, especially the big stuff. If NASA were the White House, I might be the equivalent of Monica Lewinski."

Ignoring the laughs from the officers, Dempsey acknowledged, "Okay, bad comparison, but my uncle—the man who raised me—would be the equivalent of Al Gore or Dick Cheney. He called me not ten minutes ago to tell me. He thought I might be able to reach my little girl by phone. He saw what we on Earth won't be able to see, or feel, for a few more minutes, if even then."

"And what exactly is that?" Thomas asked condescendingly.

"Our sun has, for lack of a better term, exploded. It is going to consume our planet, and there's nothing we can do to stop it. We, on the daylight side of the earth, are the lucky ones. We'll be gone in an instant. Those on the other side of the world, where it's night, they will have to suffer the burn-through."

"That's horse shit," said Thomas. "You take us for monkeys because we work security. I'm retired from the FBI, Galileo. I paid enough attention in science class to know that our sun is too small of a star for that shit. When the sun dies, it will cool—not explode."

"You're right," Dempsey answered, as he craned his neck to try to see the outdoor pool area. "But we changed all that. And by 'we,' I don't mean NASA; I mean humans."

"Thomas," one of the guards interjected, "can we just take this joker to the office? I got to be at my daughter's recital in half an hour."

Dempsey began to cry.

"Oh, man," he slurred. "I don't want to spend my last minute lecturing you all on deuterium atoms, neutrinos, and photons. The sun is one big gas ball of nuclear fusion."

"And you're saying we destroyed it?"

"I'm saying we fed it."

He searched the pool area through the glass windows behind him. The long Led Zeppelin song was winding down.

"Who knows about all of this? Just your uncle?" asked Thomas.

"The last few presidents. High-ranking officials. Oh, and several prisoners at Guantanamo Bay."

"Say what?"

"I'd been working, low level, on what I thought was a solar orbiter to launch in a couple of years. That's what we, and the rest of the world, were told. In actuality, we had secretly launched an unmanned device years ago. Not long after Saddam Hussein launched his."

"Get the fuck—"

"The 'weapon of mass destruction.' He sure did have one, but not the type the government told the world about. Made some Russian scientists rich beyond their wildest dreams. Took them decades to refine. Of course, they never thought he'd actually launch it. But he did—right out in the desert, just as our troops went in, in March 2003."

The men looked at each other.

"Ironic that Bush was actually right, but no one will be alive to know it," said Dempsey. "We sent one up a year later, faster and more advanced than theirs. Tried to catch it and neutralize it."

"You telling me it took all those years to reach the sun?" Thomas asked with a sigh.

"You should have paid closer attention in science class, Thomas. But our device failed. It sent us a feed of Saddam's transporter launching its payload. Then the sun flared, and it all went black. That's when my uncle called me."

"If any of this is true, it could just be some basic malfunction in NASA's device. Maybe a broken camera or something," said Thomas.

"Nope," said a drowsy Dempsey as he broke away from the officers and ran for the pool area. He blasted through the doorway, right past the towel girl, with the guards in pursuit. The sunlight hit his eyes as the sharks darted about in the tank. He went right for the aquarium and the warm, glistening pool that surrounded it.

Dana's picture was all he could think about. He spotted it bobbing on the surface of the water, heading toward the flapping filter door.

He had not been in a pool, river, lake, or ocean since he was six years old, but he ran in like a surfer. The security team stopped at the edge, probably not wanting to get their suits wet. He splashed furiously as he tried to reach the soaked photo. People were yelling and using their hands as visors so they could see what the commotion was about.

Dempsey—tired, impaired, and out of breath—grabbed the picture just before it could be sucked into the filter. He looked around the pool area for Kalela.

There she stood in the bright sun, no drink tray in hand, a phone to her ear. She smiled at Dempsey and raised the Samsung Galaxy to show him.

He looked down at the wet and wrinkled image of his little girl.

Then, they were all gone.

# MY FAVORITE PET
## EMERSON ADAIR

Everyone starts somewhere before the Howler takes over. I started in Vegas.

People think Vegas means riding high and living in the fast lane. The trouble with life in the fast lane is that no one likes getting back in the slow lane, and it hurts like hell when someone shoves you back down.

For a long time, I was just a joe waiting tables by day and losing my extra change by night. Then I got the bright idea to play something new. And wouldn't you know it? I made a fortune in roulette—$25,682.

*Like it matters now.*

The first night, I went from a measly fifty-seven bucks to a thousand. I didn't really have a system except to stick to red or black—no specific numbers. Things got even better the second night, and I walked out with a full five grand and change. But it was the third night when I really started loosening up. It only took one big bet on red twenty-one to hit thirty grand.

But after three misses, I decided not to press Lady Luck any further. With more than twenty-five thousand dollars to my name, I was already making plans. No more walking around like a bum for me. The next day, I was going to use my newfound wealth to buy a car. If I planned it right, I might even have a couple thousand left over.

I hit the bar. Four shots later, the whole joint was drinking a round on me, and the girls just couldn't get enough. It didn't seem to bother them that I was scrawnier than a lamp post with the face of an orangutan. Some people will do anything for a piece of someone else's good fortune.

Walking home wasn't too hard. It's pretty easy to walk drunk when you've got a looker under each arm. Strays scattered left and right, and even the alley cats had trouble taking my singing. But I didn't care. Neither did the chicks. They were too busy picking my pockets.

And that's when he showed up. Roscoe. My favorite pet. That mangy little mutt had the worst timing. He followed me to work once. I lost a whole tray of drinks on the patio because of that dog. One hundred sixty-eight dollars in liquor off my check and flushed down the drain. Roscoe got the beating of his life for that. And yet he still kept coming back.

**Howler Fact #1:** You don't have to be a Howler to carry the disease.

That's right: disease. What? You thought that you just magically joined us once you were bitten or scratched? Everything follows a process. Everything happens for a reason.

There are all sorts of animals that carry the disease: bears, wolves, dogs, cats, snakes. I met this one girl who was infected by a bird in her yard. Problem is, most beasts just look rabid, and who bothers to check what they actually had after the poor brutes are shot? Most people just burn the carcass and move on.

I had to admit—even as drunk as I was—that Roscoe looked pretty bad that night. His head hung down, and his tongue was lathered with drool that dripped to the ground in thick globs. He looked mangier than normal, and his eyes were glazed.

At first, I thought he'd gotten into another scrap with the local pack of strays. It sure seemed like he'd been pummeled into submission. But the closer he got—and the stronger the scent of blood grew—I started to realize this wasn't the same dog I was used to. Roscoe was cheerful. He never dragged himself along like he was drunk as a lord. He always pranced up like the happiest idiot in the world.

He was my favorite pet.

But that night, he was something else. That night, he'd feasted on blood. But even though he was physically satiated, he continued the hunt—driven by the disease coursing through his body.

**Howler Fact #2:** Howl is different from rabies.

Rabies is a virus. Howl is a bacterium. Rabies makes an animal mad—makes it lose its mind before the virus kills it. Howl heightens your instincts, makes you a hunter. Some assume that means you'll attack anything, just like you would with rabies. That's not so. The attack instinct is there, but you also know when to quit. You know how to survive.

I guess Roscoe figured a drunken man hanging off a couple of backstabbing whores was as good a prey as any. He didn't even bother to growl—just went straight for the jugular. And every day, I cuss myself out for putting my arm in the way.

He was stronger than I expected. He knocked me flat on my back. The thieving whores shrieked and made a run for the street. Roscoe must have decided I would be too much work. He let go of my arm and took down the first one he could reach. She only got one good scream out before he ripped her throat open. Too bad it wasn't the one with my wallet.

Being drunk generally means a quiet getaway is out of the question. Not that it mattered. Roscoe was too busy stuffing his face to notice. I stumbled the rest of the way to my apartment and locked myself in. My arm hurt like hell, but then, so did my head. In retrospect, passing out on the couch was not the best idea. Especially since the bite was already infected by morning.

**Howler Fact #3:** Howl can be treated.

You fight it with antibiotics, just like every other kind of bacterium. The problem is you've only got about twelve to twenty-four hours before it's too late. That's just dandy for smart rich folk who can afford a trip to the ER. But for poor idiots like me, well . . .

At first, I doused the bite in any and every kind of alcohol I had. The swelling in my arm went down, but now I was feverish and hallucinating. Three whole days later, I dragged myself to the clinic. My senses were sharpening too. I could hear the doc's breathing and his old joints cracking as he probed the bite. He smelled musty and sour—not very appetizing. But I hadn't eaten in days.

Wait! What was I thinking? Eat the doc? *Eat* him? That couldn't be right. But the Howler was rising now. A chubby young nurse came in to take a blood sample. Not too fat. Tender, sweet, plentiful meat. It was taking everything I had not to lunge for her throat.

**Howler Fact #4:** The Howler can be managed.

It's not really a matter of timing for the Howler. It's about choice and control. The urge to rise is always there. It's not always easy to shift. The full moon makes the change easier. Something in the magnetics works on the animal brain. But an experienced Howler can change any time they want. It's just safer and easier to wait for night.

It didn't take much to change that first time. The prick of the nurse's needle triggered a fight instinct. Before I even knew what had happened, the doctor's body was on the floor and his head was bouncing outside in the hall. The nurse was on her back, gurgling, with her stomach slit open. Yes, she was very tender. Somewhere buried under the Howler, what was left of my sanity realized she wasn't even dead yet.

The armed security guard tried to take me down. You'd think he would know to aim for the head against something that big. It wasn't long before the whole clinic was empty and the Howler was satisfied.

I vaguely remember a crouching canine-like figure looking back at me from the glass doors. The arms were freakishly long, ending with giant hands covered in blood. There was dark brown fur all over it—so dark it was almost black. But the head was what caught my attention. It was like a wolf's. I guess that's how werewolves got their name. The funny thing is, past the appearance and the howling, Howlers are nothing like wolves. Wolves hunt in packs; Howlers keep to themselves.

**Howler Fact #5:** Shedding can be avoided.

The first shedding was one of the most disgusting things I'd ever felt. It was like someone had taken the skin off a bleeding animal and thrown it over me. You have to grab and rip the skin off. And just like the myths say, you come out naked and bloody. I found out later that the shedding stops when you gain more control.

I tried to stay in Vegas, but the city's just too busy. There was too much to seduce the Howler. I decided to head to the Sierra Nevada. But I had one thing to take care of before I left.

I found him in another alley near the Strip. He was feasting on a large cat and her kittens. It only took one swift blow to the back of the neck. I burned the remains in a metal trashcan.

Poor old Roscoe. My favorite pet.

# THE END
## *MELISSA ALGOOD*

I was ten when most of the human race was wiped from the planet. For a while, it was just Dad and me. Then winter came and never went away. We shared the last can of beef stew on my eleventh birthday, and then left the southern shores of Washington.

Forever.

The frozen rain pounded our frail bodies until we found an abandoned, rust-covered 2020 Chevy on the feeder of the highway. Dad said it would be good luck since it was made the same year I was born. He had me watch as he pulled some wires from under the steering wheel, twisted the red and yellow ones, and started the truck. Dad smiled at me. We headed south. Our powerful enemy, sleet, poured in through the window Dad had broken.

My voice turned into a howl as it was ravaged by the wind. "How much farther?"

Dad turned to me. Ice coated his auburn beard. "We're heading to Mexico."

"Yeah, but how far is that?"

"Didn't you learn that in school?"

I recalled school. My buddies and I would sit in the back of class shooting spit balls at the teacher and have pizza-eating contests at lunch. I didn't remember what potato chips tasted like, much less where exactly Mexico was on a map. "Maybe?"

"Well, we're in Oregon. So . . . " His gloved hands gripped the steering wheel of the truck we'd stolen. Maybe it wasn't really stealing, since the owner had died. Dad cast his dark irises upon the lonely road ahead of us. It was a look I'd never seen until it was only the two of us. I didn't have a word to define his expression. The endless search for a way to describe the sadness in his eyes made me wish I'd paid more attention in language arts class.

-$-

A few weeks after the Chevy ran out of gas and we couldn't find any more, we started walking. According to Dad, we were atop Summer Lake when we met John, who looked as haggard and worn as Dad's cough. I couldn't remember when Dad's lungs started to expel a thick yellow substance with black dots intermingled with the phlegm, but it kept him from sleeping by the time we added to our family. As time went on, I found out how important grown-ups' jobs had been before everything went away. John promised to get us across the mountains. After all, he had majored in sports medicine and was an avid rock climber. We should've made sure he meant that he'd get us both to Nevada alive.

Dad's face had turned white as flour by the time we were halfway down. "How much longer, John?"

Our guide stopped and looked over his shoulder. "We'll be there by nightfall, Hank." His light eyes scanned Dad. "You need to take a break?"

"No. I can't spend another night on this rock."

John nodded and headed southeast, but I held back with Dad. "You okay?"

"Don't worry about me. It'll all be over soon."

Nightfall came, extinguishing the final, barely existent beams of light, and we still had a few more hours of ground to cover. "We gotta make camp," John said.

"No, keep going."

"But you can't—"

Dad's voice turned into a growl. "You have to keep going." He turned to me. "Take this." He unzipped his coat.

"No way! You need it."

"No. I don't." He pulled his faded-yellow down coat over my own. "These, too." He opened the knapsack that hung over his boney shoulder and handed me three hardback novels tied together with twine. They were all by George Orwell, my namesake. I could faintly recall my mother's singsong voice telling me that only an English professor would name all his children after authors. I didn't know what she meant. Maybe that's because I never had the chance to read Ray Bradbury or Emily Brontë.

"Dad, you don't have to—"

His index finger glided along the side of my face. Still to this day, it is the coldest thing I've ever felt. A gust of wind filled the space between us, and he clung to a rock on the side of the mountain. He buried his face in his hands. "George . . . "

"What?" I bent my knees so our faces were level. His empty eyes were glassy and half-closed. "Dad?" I shook him by his shoulders. "Dad!" A thin line of red dripped from his nose.

"We need to go," John said.

I shook my head. My brain had shattered like glass. "We'll go when he wakes up."

John pulled me up by my arm. Dark hair stuck to his forehead. "It's what he wanted. You have to live, kid."

Dad's face was blue. Maybe he could still hear me? I knew I'd never get to speak to him again, so maybe I should have taken advantage of our last moments. But I'd already said goodbye to everyone I ever loved; I couldn't do it again. My eyes were dry when I took the rope from my dad's hand. John unhooked him and intertwined the rope with mine. John and I continued down the mountain.

-$-

John and I made it to Vegas three years later, shortly after I'd turned sixteen. At least, I thought I was sixteen. It had been impossible to gauge time since the sun had been blocked out by an endless haze all these years. Apparently, Vegas used to be a pretty lively place. Now it was only the two of us.

John extended his left arm. His black-leather-gloved hand pointed at a structure covered in snow, ice, and sludge. It had a square base and shot up into the gray sky like an arrow. "See that?"

"Yeah," I muttered, not finding it entirely impressive.

He looked over at me and steam rushed out of his mouth with his words. "That's as close as you'll ever come to the Eiffel Tower."

"What's that?"

He threw his head back and laughed. "Seriously? You don't know what that is, kid?"

"I was in fourth grade . . . when it all . . . you know."

More to the wind than to me, John said, "Forgot about that."

"I didn't get to graduate college like you."

"Technically, I was eighteen credits shy, but who's counting anymore?"

"So, what was it anyway? The tower?"

"It was a great architectural feat way back when it was built. The real one is in Paris, France. This one is a replica."

I racked my limited vocabulary attempting to pinpoint the meaning of this new word. "What's a replica?"

"It's a copy of something. They built copies of famous landmarks and places here. It was the playground of the rich and the place the poor came to, to dream of getting wealthy fast."

"Did you ever come here? Before?"

"When I was your age, with my parents, so I couldn't have any fun." He punched me in the arm, which made me feel ten again. For a moment, I was back with my friends and I could feel the sun on my skin. "Maybe I was younger; I didn't have a full beard like you, kid."

I rubbed my own chin. My cotton gloves pulled on the coarse hairs that grew along my jaw. I wondered if it was the same color as my Dad's. I had yet to find a mirror void of a thick film of ash and ice. It would be awkward to ask John. Besides, Dad was pretty much dead already when they met; how could I ask him to compare us? "What do you mean: you couldn't have any fun?"

"It used to be a city built for adults and all their vices."

"Vices?"

He stopped in the middle of the road and rested his hands on my shoulders. "It's like this, kid. We're walking on something they called the Strip. It had a bunch of casinos, hookers, and whatever else you wanted to help you forget about the life you were living."

My eyes crisscrossed the buildings blanketed in snow that had turned the same eerie color as the sky. They were so tall I didn't know if we were still walking on the earth, or if we were really dead and walking in the atmosphere. My older sister once told me that hell was hot, but maybe she was wrong and it was so cold that the blood in your body turned into icicles. If there was ever a time for escape, it was now. I would have given anything just to have another minute of life: belly full, showers in hot water, my parents kissing me goodnight. I couldn't think of an instance when I would have chosen to avoid what I had, not now when all I could do was hold on to the few memories left in my brain.

I'd do anything to see leaves rustling in the summer breeze above me. Instead, I found myself surrounded by desolate gray. And death.

"What's a hooker, John?"

"Jesus, kid." He chuckled and looked down at the ground before he turned his brown eyes back to mine. "I'm so glad I got to sleep with a chick before all of this happened. I promise you—right here, right now—I will find you a cute teenage girl if it's the last thing I do."

He'd made comments like this before. Yet in the years we'd traveled as a pair, we'd never come across another soul. I'd lost hope that I'd ever get another kiss from a girl like Jenna, who'd once snuck behind the gym with me. Her lips had tasted better than strawberry ice cream and made my body feel like I was on a roller coaster. For some reason, the lack of girls made me think of something my brother always said: "Ignorance is bliss." My gaze turned back to the buildings around us. "Right now, I'd be happy if I could get something to eat."

John tilted his head to the nearest building with the least amount of ice covering the front. We took the pickaxes hanging from the sides of our packs and hammered the sheet of frozen water that encased our would-be shelter. I don't know if it took minutes, hours, or what, but I was exhausted by the time we broke through and hobbled inside.

It looked like every other building I'd broken into: torn up. As I gazed about the still space, I recalled the times Mom would ask, "Another tornado run through your room, George?" I didn't find it funny then— although it had always made Dad laugh—and I still didn't. The only tornado I'd ever seen was the one in *The Wizard of Oz*. That had been so long ago I wouldn't have been able to tell you why she was walking down that yellow brick road, even if you offered me a bacon cheeseburger with french fries. But there was something in the room that made me forget all about Mom's smile and fried food.

The ceiling.

John nudged me with his elbow and held up the kerosene lamp to cast more light above us. "Pretty cool, huh, kid?"

People covered the dome that my eyes scanned. I assumed it was paint since I couldn't touch it, but it had every color I remembered from before the sky clouded over forever. And more. Babies with rosy cheeks, wings, and harps. Women in pastel flowing robes, their long, wavy hair floating behind them. Men with long beards that reminded me of Dad. The robin's egg blue was a beautiful contrast against the puffy white clouds that resembled whip cream.

"It's . . . it's . . . " Again, I couldn't find the appropriate word, and for just a moment, I felt a loosening in my chest. As if I'd been holding my breath ever since my family died, along with everyone else I had ever known.

John's face sagged. It was like he'd aged twenty years since I'd met him. "It's nice to see, but I don't even know if there's a point anymore."

"What do you mean?"

"Well, that's not gonna feed us." He nodded his head up at the painting. "Or start a fire. I don't even know who they're supposed to be. Maybe they were once really famous people, but no one knows who they are anymore. So, what's the point of even seeing it?"

I thought about the fact that John might die before me and then I'd really be alone. As a kid, I had dreamed of being the only person left and having the opportunity to eat all the candy I wanted, drive any car through the streets, and of course, not go to school. Once John was gone, I'd be living a nightmare. He never talked about his time alone before he met Dad and me, which made me believe that it wasn't great. "We don't know who they are, but it is still important. I'm glad I saw it."

"Why?"

"It means we're still alive."

John shot me a smile. "You know the girls aren't gonna come to life while you're asleep and take your virginity or anything, kid."

Maybe I blushed. I used to do that whenever I was embarrassed, but I hadn't thawed yet. "I'll take anything that will keep my mind off . . . all this." I gazed about the wreckage of the hotel lobby.

"You know the drill, kid."

I nodded. He started pulling all the wooden furniture to the center of the lobby and breaking it down with his ax. I filled the pot that I retrieved from my backpack with snow and then took out my own ax and helped John. The hotel bar took up a whole wall to the left of a reception desk, which held a half dozen useless computers. Several dozen matchbooks, which were akin to diamonds in the apocalypse, filled a fishbowl atop the bar. But not a drop of alcohol.

"Damnit!" John slammed his hand against a lever that once dispensed beer. "I guess he figured if he was going out, he'd go out wasted." His boot kicked the lone skeleton with frayed rags clinging to its bones. It must have been the last person alive, since it hadn't been dragged to the edge of town and burned with the rest of the charred bodies.

"Maybe there's some in one of those little fridges."

"Little . . . what?"

"You know, the ones that are in each room, with all the really good candy in them?" Whenever my family had gone to a hotel, we kids were expressly forbidden from opening them, much less consuming their contents. But the idea of dying without ever having a beer depressed me. I'd already missed so much of what many teenagers experienced; I didn't want to miss out on what adults did too.

"You're smarter than you look, kid. Let's eat first, though."

After the snow came to a boil, I held a cloth over our thermoses. John slowly poured the liquid through the cloth as we both attempted to keep our faces free from the steam. It felt great letting it surround your whole face, but steam could burn worse than boiling water. At least, according to John it could. He took the thinnest rabbit in existence out of his pack, and I skinned it. We each took a share and let it cook in our respective thermos before we indulged in rabbit stew.

In my sixteen years, it was the best thing I'd ever cooked.

After John gulped his last bit of rabbit, he asked, "You wanna check out the rooms now, kid?"

I nodded and threw my bag over my shoulders. I never left it alone. Not only because I might find something that I'd want to take with me—like food—but because it held the books Dad had given me before he died. I had yet to untie the twine Dad had wrapped around them, but they never left my side.

"Where should we start, kid?"

"The bottom floors are probably already cleaned out."

"Wanna try twenty-seven? Since that's how old I am? I think."

I nodded, happy to know that I wasn't the only man left on Earth who didn't know what year it was anymore. "Then we gotta try sixteen too."

"Anything you want. Just stick by my side."

"Yeah," I laughed. At least, that's what it felt like, even though the sound was deep and raw. "Don't want to lose your only friend in the world."

John's large chocolate-colored eyes faltered. He gazed at me, but then again, his eyes were blank. It was as if he saw everyone he'd lost in me, just like I saw everyone who had died in him. "I'll never lose you, George. Never."

He'd only ever called me my real name a few times. When he said "George," it took away all my pain and replaced it with something else I couldn't name. I didn't know how to answer, so I just nodded.

We were both pretty pissed when there wasn't anything to drink on the sixteenth floor and we'd nearly torn our lungs out with the climb. Still, we made the trek up to the twenty-seventh floor. Our effort was rewarded. The third room we came to had the wine.

The warming effect of the fridge, which was supposed to keep them cold but had lost power, managed to keep the delicious contents from freezing.

John handed me a bottle the length of my hand. "Would have preferred vodka, but you know what they say about beggars, kid?"

I twisted it open, sniffed it, and threw my head back. It tasted thick, like syrup, but it didn't taste sweet at all.

"Whoa, kid! Take it slow. You're not used to the stuff."

I swallowed the last drop from my bottle and shrugged.

"Want another?" I nodded, and he handed me a bottle. "Let's save the last couple, you think?"

"I bet we can find more."

"I'll take that bet."

It was four more rooms before we cheered with joy again.

We returned downstairs to the lobby, because we could build another fire and we knew where the exit was. I leaned against my backpack and finished off another tiny bottle of wine—head spinning, body numb . . . like the times I would go on a roller coaster with my brother. "I feel . . . weird . . ."

John laughed. "That's called drunk, kid."

"Feels pretty good."

"Try and remember that tomorrow morning."

"What happens tomorrow?"

The light from the fire brought a lively glow to John's face. "You'll see."

It wasn't long after that my eyelids became heavier than stone. With my backpack as a pillow, I curled up and fell asleep. But I didn't dream. I saw nothing but endless darkness whenever I closed my eyes.

-$-

That night though, I felt something on my hand. It was warm and wet. The sensation made me slowly open my eyes. It's coat was jet black and shone against the light behind it. The light was bright, almost like the sun, and it nearly blinded me. When my eyes came into focus and saw the creature next to me, I screamed. The animal's eyes were black as coal, its tongue pink as my sister's ballet costume, and its tail wagged quickly. I didn't scream because it was scary but because it had been so long since I'd seen one.

John bolted upright. He pulled me up off the floor and back against the reception desk we'd partially dismembered earlier. My leg caught on my bag, scattering the contents in front of the dog. Two flashlight beams zeroed in on us. John stood in front of me and raised the kerosene lamp as he called out, "Are you alone?"

A woman's voice came from one of the flashlight beams. "Are you?"

"Asked you first."

I could hear the girl breathing. It was quick and harsh as if she'd just run a mile. "Yes."

"How long?" John asked.

"Few years. What about you?"

John's hand gripped tighter around my shoulder before he said, "Been the two of us for a while now."

"What did you do to our dog?"

"Nothing. He's here," John said.

"I heard a scream."

"Your dog woke us up. Call him if you don't believe me."

Another, softer voice sang out from the other flashlight. "Lucky!" The black lab turned back toward the girls.

49

A few moments passed, filled with girl-whispers, before John asked, "How'd you get here?"

"Walked. Hoped it would be warmer. You?"

"Same, from Seattle."

"We're from Detroit."

"So what's your name?"

The older girl lowered her flashlight from our faces and cast the light on her own. Her dark hair hung past her shoulders. She wore a scarf and hat tucked into her parka and hood. Her lips were pale and matched the rest of her face, as if she'd been drained of life. When they parted, she said, "Anne."

John lowered the kerosene lamp to the side and said, "John."

"Who's your friend?"

John looked over at me and nodded. I turned to the first girl I'd seen in five years. "George."

Anne had already maneuvered around the remains of our fire, with Lucky on her heels. "This is my sister, Brenda."

Brenda's long brown hair was in a single braid that lay on her right shoulder. The coat she wore was once red, it's crimson glow still obvious underneath the ash. She wasn't close enough for me to be sure, but Brenda looked to be just a few inches shorter than me. "How old are you, George?"

"Sixteen. You?"

"Fourteen."

Next to us, John and Anne continued interrogating each other. That's how I found out they were all that was left of a group that had been slowly starving to death. They'd gone out on their own when violence broke out and the remaining people tried to eat Lucky. Anne had just rushed a sorority when the earth died, along with the rest of her dreams. Lucky moved in circles around the four of us, sniffing and digging randomly at the floor.

Brenda's gaze followed him, stopping at my backpack. "Are those books?"

"Yeah."

"Can you read them to me?" She gazed at me with eyes brighter than the moon. "It's been so long since anyone has."

I turned to John, who was telling Anne about his time in college. I figured if he felt safe, then I should too; I leaned against the wall and slid to the floor. Brenda handed the books to me. I took a deep breath and unwrapped the twine. "Which one do you want me to read?"

"Which one is your favorite?"

I looked at the titles and not a single memory came forward. "I don't . . . "

"How about this one?" She sat, legs crossed and Lucky settling beside her. "I always wanted to see a farm."

I ran my finger along the skinny, battered spine. "I'm pretty sure it doesn't end happy. It's just like everything else that's left."

"Well." Brenda leaned in closer to me. "Let's hope it does this time."

The book's weight in my hands calmed me. It reminded me of when Dad would read to me before I fell asleep. Brenda rested her head on my shoulder as I flipped past the title page and started from the beginning.

# REVERSE SLOT MACHINE
## *GWEN HART*

Wayne spotted her as soon as she came up the open-air escalator from the Fashion Show mall. She was sixty-plus, was a little too plump, and had the sleeves of her brand-new, patterned jacket carefully rolled up. Her purple, crinkled-cotton shirt and capris pants were the kind advertised as "perfect for travel" in the back of *AARP The Magazine*. Her short haircut didn't flatter her face, but it was artfully frosted and coiffed. She sported a pair of those expensive glasses that change tint depending on the light.

Wayne fiddled with the machine. He only had a few moments to set it up properly once he saw a mark. Some people thought the key to being successful was the pompadour. Others relied on glitzy outfits. There was, of course, the singing to be considered, although those who couldn't carry a tune simply lip-synced. The hips were an issue as well: Could they swivel? Could they shake?

Wayne knew he had it all—the whole package—but he felt none of those things were the most important, most crucial factor. The secret was something that couldn't be taught or bought—the musical instinct to know which song to play for which woman. What would touch her heart and make her forget about all her cares, including her purse, her wallet, and her jewelry?

Wayne was a master of matching the song to the lady. He instinctively knew which tune to cue up on his portable karaoke machine—"All

Shook Up," "Burning Love," "Don't Be Cruel," or the slower "Release Me," "Love Me Tender," or "Are You Lonesome Tonight?"

This woman in the purple outfit was definitely "Teddy Bear"—sweet and nonthreatening. His fingers nimbly flipped the CD, punched the buttons, and adjusted his microphone headset.

He jumped up and stretched out his arms as she approached, swinging his hips to the fast beat from the machine. Just as he'd suspected, she stepped quickly into his open arms, ready and willing to be serenaded, twirled, and dipped.

*Reverse slot machine.* That was what Wayne called it. While they danced, he'd reach into her pockets, relieving her of the cash she'd have fed into those rigged gadgets in Caesars Palace or the Bellagio. He was doing her a favor, really. She'd never get as much out of those inanimate objects as she'd get out of a dance with the King himself.

The song was magic while it lasted. Wayne sneered and growled through the whole two minutes, dancing so hard his forehead broke out in a sweat. When the final chords sounded, he spun her back into the crowd, blowing her a kiss. He could feel the weight of the loot in the hidden back pocket of his gold-thread-embellished jacket as he watched her float down the open-air escalator and out onto the busy sidewalk of the Strip. This was why he stayed here, year after year. He believed in Vegas—in making people's dreams come true.

-$-

Louise spotted him right away—saw him sizing her up from behind his corny white-plastic sunglasses at the end of the elevated walkway that linked the Fashion Show mall to the Las Vegas Strip. He was sitting on a folding director's chair behind a cardboard sign that read, *Will sing and dance for a kiss!* He had greasy black hair and a potbelly that threatened to break the golden threads cinching his costume together. She had a tube of lipstick, a Starbucks loyalty card, and a few singles in her pockets. Her wrists and fingers clattered with plastic dime-store jewelry molded to look like turquoise. She'd left her purse locked in the cute little safe in the hotel room that you could set with your own combination. She'd gone to the mall food court for a cheap dinner and some window-shopping. She hadn't wanted the temptation of her credit cards burning a hole in her pocket while she was in there. She'd already blown enough of her savings on the flight from Omaha, hotel room, new eyeglasses, and three outfits for the trip.

Louise had won a laser-printed certificate for first place in the over-sixty dance competition at the community center back in Bad Luck Lake, Iowa. She followed the out-of-shape Elvis's lead—even when it didn't make much sense—carefully side-stepping the director's chair and being mindful not to hit the metal-and-glass barriers at the edge of the walkway when he spun her in a crazy circle.

He had picked the corniest song of all, "Teddy Bear." She tried to make it look as if she laughed with him, and not at him, as he twirled her around and around—a hand on her hip, at her shoulder, circling her wrist, reaching into her pocket. She even lifted her arms up, waving her hands above her head to the beat to make it easier for him.

A few people stopped to gape. They must have been new to town, not yet dazzled by the sinking pirate ship or exploding volcano. It was probably their first fake Elvis, their first glimpse of a girl gone Vegas wild. Two young women with smartphones were recording the scene. She threw her head back and chuckled out loud as the jowly singer growled and snapped at her neck. She could see he was really enjoying himself, trying so hard to be cool that he was breaking into a sweat. In his mind, it was 1957 and he really was the King, making some sixteen-year-old teenybopper swoon.

She left him with a jaunty angle to his chin and four crisp dollar bills and a few pieces of costume jewelry in his pockets. She was glad she could offer him a short respite from sitting on the uncomfortable chair and watching people's sweaty, blistered feet tramp by in gladiator sandals. This was exactly why she kept coming back here, year after year.

Down on the Strip, Louise took her time. She paused to watch the fountains at the Bellagio dance to "Luck Be a Lady." She was in no hurry; half the pleasure was in the anticipation. After the song finished, she strolled into the Bellagio and locked herself in an ornate stall in the ladies' room. Carefully, she unrolled the left sleeve of her purple jacket. She looked admiringly at the lovely pieces she'd acquired: a rose-gold ring with *peace* inscribed on the band, a sterling-silver money clip in the shape of a horse head with a diamond chip for the eye, and over one hundred dollars in various bills. Louise had to admit, she'd underestimated him. The over-the-hill Elvis had done some good work that day.

Carefully, she swept the treasures off the back of the commode and put them in her pocket. She freshened her lipstick in the gilt bathroom mirror and left one of the five-dollar bills for the attendant. Now to put her plan into action. She headed back to the pawn shop she'd seen. With her earnings, she was ready to try her luck. She made her way to the floor of the Bellagio. She believed in Vegas—in making her dreams come true.

# PEACEFUL PERSPECTIVE
*CHRISTINA MORALES*

"No, I don't know anyone in Vegas," I answer my sixteen-year-old son.

"Then why are you going there alone?"

"I won't be alone. Some girls that I grew up with decided that we should all get together there," I answer. "Because that's kind of a central location."

"Define . . . 'grew up with,' Mom?"

"Let me see; we went to elementary, junior high, and high school together. Then, we all went our own way for college or military service. We reconnected through Facebook, because we all live in different cities across the country. We chat, call each other, and when it so happens that we are in the same town or state together, we act like kids, gossip, laugh, and you get the picture, right?"

"Sounds like old lady fun." My son flips his medium-length brown hair out of his eyes and gives me one of his perfect smiles. He's beautiful in a way that few can imagine.

"That's the idea."

-$-

That is the idea. That is the plan. I am leaving for an all-girl vacation in Vegas with a group of women that I have not seen in almost twenty years. Our strategy is to get together for breakfast every day and pick shows that we want to see and choose things we want to do. With nine women, there will be a partner for everyone's interest. At night, our common interest in alcohol will unite us at one of the many hotel bars.

As we play musical beds in the hotel room on that first evening, a realization comes to me.

*It's amazing how surrounding yourself with women who know your backstory frees you to enjoy the "real-time" moments as they happen.*

Do I have to tell anyone that I am on my second marriage? No, and because we come from the same small town, they even know the details of the first crash and burn. I know theirs, too. What we don't know or choose not to share isn't important. We are unencumbered by our baggage and full of mutual respect for each other's journey.

Like most women in their forties, I have mastered a few things. I give myself moments of self-care that are owed to me from my younger years, when I never slept or peed without a baby somewhere close by—at times, too close. I have come to believe that the extra pudge around the middle is a sign of a life well lived and it makes my body as soft as my heart—call it *body-n-heart balance*. I have also learned not to take things personally because I am not the central motivation behind most people's actions. In all, I take the plot twists in life gracefully . . . with a few exceptions.

It has been a hard year. My sister passed away, and in the way that families often do when the glue that binds them comes undone, things went to hell. One sister died, and the other two went from being friends to being barely amicable. My grandmother—my father's mother—also passed away. She was the last thing that bound me to the man I had lost a decade earlier. To see her face was to see Dad. It was difficult to say good-bye.

My marriage is coming out of its greatest slump in seventeen years. Constant work-related travel made for long absences and poor communication between the man whom I knew as my best friend and me. We had neglected that which made our relationship so special. We've survived, though not unscathed. The marriage was battle worn and loosely tethered when we discovered that our son was no longer in the mood to tolerate the business of life. My beautiful boy's struggle with mental illness dragged him through a half-year's worth of outpatient hospitalization and medications. Finally, we found one that made him feel only remotely healthy. Yeah, hard is a most accurate description of my life this year.

Question: So, when you are exhausted and emotionally beat down, is it a good time to run away to Vegas?

Answer: Well, duh?

-$-

As we get ready for our first nightly reunion at the lobby bar, Becky looks in the mirror appreciatively and says, "This is my time. This moment is about me and getting my needs met."

Her strength, her beauty, and the way her hair sways make me crush on her a little. I'm straight, but she is the embodiment of power. Her story is strong, and it tells of a woman who had to build herself from the ground up. She is well educated and married to a man who appreciates her for herself. She is so happy that she positively glows.

I remember what she went through in school for being tall and strong. Boys were cruel to her. She is a girl no more, and the woman in her is capable of taming the character of even the toughest man. It is funny how we become either powerful or weak as a result of our childhood years. It is a choice we make, and yet, somehow, it isn't a choice we make. Sometimes, we just don't know how to stay down.

Four of us have arrived thus far, and the first night becomes the first morning as we're finishing off the drinking with breakfast when the late flight of a few more friends finally arrives. Afterward, we gamble. We lose. We win. We laugh. We lose and win, again.

My official roomie for the week is Eliza, and she arrives on day two. The other girls have another room now. Eliza enlisted before high school graduation and is still *Army strong*. She is powerful, gorgeous, and brilliant. The kid in her has been gone since basic training. She works hard, lives hard, and amazingly enough . . . prays harder. Training made her a weapon, but God dictates her aim. She is a testament to order and conditioning.

Eliza's attraction to the *Sex in the City* slot machine is hilarious at best. As we leave a show on night three, she sees it from across the room, past the mostly undressed girls dancing on the bars. Mr. Big, surrounded by neon pink, calls to Eliza, and she slides another hundred-dollar bill into the slot machine.

Mandy and I sit at the bar and laugh as we wait for Eliza's gambling needs to be met. Mandy is the most like me and my cousin to boot. The biggest difference is that she likes people and I don't—not while sober anyway.

"So . . . how would you tell your friends if your daughter were a stripper in Vegas?" I ask Mandy, as the girl on this side of the bar removes a belt that didn't cover much. The dancer bends over, making her butt cheeks jiggle for her admirers.

Mandy considers the question for a bit, wearing a sly grin. "Hmm . . . proudly, I guess. When I wiggle like that, I'm lucky to get another Coach purse. She's making a paycheck."

Of course, I laugh at that. We were raised with an incredible work ethic. A paycheck beats unemployment any day of the week. So I say, "Kind of along the same lines as the guy in the bar last night who prostituted himself to us so we would vote for his daughter when she came up for the swimsuit competition?"

"They were paying her with alcohol. That doesn't count," she says.

"Alcohol is expensive. A night at the bar can cost upward of forty dollars, and that's if you're a cheap drinker. In my book, that girl got paid."

"Her daddy whored himself to you so you would get all the people screaming for her," says Mandy.

Grimacing at my own behavior, I try to make a witty retort. "Shut up. I only recruited the menopause votes."

We give the girls at the bar respectful looks for their hard work—and for their undoubted willingness to give up sweets to look like that.

"You danced well last night, Chris," Mandy comments.

"Tonight, it's your turn."

"No!" Eliza screams from the slots behind us. She is talking to Mr. Big. "You hate me, but I love you so much!"

Mandy and I look at each other. We are entirely sober even though we may not sound like it.

"Let's go back to our hotel to wait for the others so we can get a drink," says Mandy.

-$-

That night, just the two of us watch *Jersey Boys*, a musical about the Four Seasons. The other women wanted a show called *Thunder from Down Under*. Surely, they will need a drink once they have had their fill of watching men dance around in G-strings. Is it even possible to get too much Thunder?

Throughout the night, texts update us that there are lap dances involved. Later, when we meet up with the "thunder" team, we note a warm, menopausal glow. I wonder if it is hot flash or G-string related. By the end of the night, I find out.

We head out on our nightly bar hunt. The sweet buzz from the foot-tall drinks that we drank permeate the atmosphere with electricity at Señor Frog's. Technically, it is already tomorrow, past one in the morning. The crowd is loud and beyond tipsy. Normal social standards are suspended for our decompression needs.

The rough year is danced away. The rhythm of the music works like a rub to make me forget my son's illness and the lifetime of vigilance to come. I put all worries aside for these lovely moments as I focus on my body, my breathing, and myself for just a beat. Anything outside of the dance is kept away by the desert moat that surrounds Vegas.

The ill-gotten, meager funds earned by stealing time from my family slide happily onto the bar. And like the money, the guilt of putting time and effort into the impossible dream of becoming a writer also fades away. There is guilt in chasing something for *me* when I should be devoting energy to my children and my marriage. The guilt may be a side effect of my upbringing.

Even if for a night, the gin-whiskey combos erase the heartbreak of losing my sister. She was the first person I ever gambled with. She took me on a girl's weekend years ago, and we had so much fun. The year of her death, I could not make the time to go with her. The alcohol dulls the ache and clears it away long enough for me to remember how much she loved this town.

The loud music drowns out the memories of sobbing in the closet when I knew my marriage was as broken as it could possibly be. The beat replaces the sting in my heart from when I cried myself to sleep those many nights. My ears take in power chords that envelop my yesterday and flush it away. Like a song, in marriage there is no going backward. The next chord comes without holding onto the last. I believe it will be better.

The women to my left and to my right might still be in high school with the way we dance. Menopause is on hold. Instead of the common hot-flash sweat, we drip with sensuality that we had forgotten we owned.

Forty years are gone by, and we make simple requests of each other. Mandy says, "Chris, let's do that humpy thing they are doing over there." I turn around and see people practically having sex on the dance floor. Well, they may actually be having sex. This *is* Vegas.

"I think I saw that on HBO one night. I'm not doing that with you." I yell over my shoulder and laugh.

The night ends, and luckily enough, we find our rooms . . . eventually.

-$-

My alarm goes off.

From her bed, my roommate, Eliza, grunts, "Christina, why do I hear the Ave Maria?"

"Shh," I say. "Go back to sleep. I'm going to church."

"Seriously?" she asks.

"Yes," I whisper.

The short walk stirs my senses. I sit through mass and become fully alive in the modern-looking church. Visitors are acknowledged, welcomed, and fed spiritually for the week to come. I rarely attend church alone. My children typically surround me. Being alone makes it possible to absorb the message thoroughly. I feel purged of the yuck and renewed with hope.

Vegas sands out the roughness, and I come away still having experienced my life, but I am now smoothed and refined.

I can see that my sister's life was well lived and not wasted. I can see that the cracks we allowed in our marriage now enable us to fill the gaps with God, goodness, and thankfulness. It was too easy to accept the blessings without recognizing the Giver. I understand that my son's illness is one of life's crosses. This one is lighter because, though it is his, he has a stronger, happier mom to help him. I am empowered by the women who remind me of where we came from and where we are. The distance traveled is remarkable—from food stamps to fur.

Vegas does not erase the year's struggles. Its bright lights, splashy scenes, and great shows merely give them a different backdrop. My everyday issues are a single bulb on the expanse of the Strip. The whole is still bright and beautiful, and the broken light is an easy fix.

Vegas is . . . peaceful. It is . . . perspective. It is peaceful perspective in the middle of a desert.

# ABSOLUTELY EQUITABLE
*VERSTANDT*

The stars slip like diamonds across the black mirror surface of the limousine as it glides along the little-known, and oft-abandoned, Alamo Road. Inside, the scent of synthetic leather is thick. The tint of the glass reflects the man's muted visage: eyes submerged in shadow and his expression grave as he watches the vast expanse of the Mojave Desert ripple seamlessly by. The bitter taste of copper lingers in his mouth, like blood. The muffled thumps emanating from the trunk settled into silence many miles past and the only sound that remains is the uneven, hypnotic churn of wheels rolling over packed dirt and loose rock. On occasion, the view of the desert outside is interrupted by a sign—faded, weather beaten, and pockmarked by random shot. White Rock, Slate Mine, Deadhorse—each road more desolate than the last. Once, a sign slipped past proclaiming that travel beyond this point is prohibited, but this particular voyage heeds no such civil calls.

After many miles spent in silent contemplation, the car slows to a halt. He looks about for a sign but sees none. He opens the door and steps out. Desert dust billows in swirling plumes around him. It stings his eyes and coats the back of his throat, making him cough. He walks to the front of the limo and taps on the glass. It slides down just a crack, and he sees the small slits of eyes peering back out at him. He can just make out the caked blood that runs down the driver's face like dried rivers in an arid valley.

"Is this it?" the man asks.

"This is it," the driver replies.

The man nods, and the window slides back up. He walks around to the front of the car and begins removing his clothes. He lays them in a pile before him until he stands nude—save for the watch about his wrist—bathed in the headlights of the limousine. He crouches and retrieves a pack of matches from his trousers. He strikes one and touches the flame to the cloth. He stands and watches as it devours the meager meal.

He turns and squints against the headlights; the silhouette of the driver is barely visible through the glare. He nods again, and the car backs up, turns around, and heads back into the desert. He watches until the light of the car is but a spark in the distance. He turns and beholds the barren road stretching out into darkness. He stares into the face of his watch. The final few seconds tick down to midnight, and he steps over the smoldering ashes, crossing the unmarked border into Las Vegas.

-$-

The screeching harmonic distortion and haunting vocals of The Jesus and Mary Chain's *Psychocandy* scream through the cheap tin speakers of the van's interior. Brandon sits on the sill and hangs out the window, his massive ape-like hand clinging to the "oh shit" handle. He pushes his face into the wind and howls like a beast on the verge of an adrenaline overdose. He bangs his fist against the side of the van over and over again, and I might have minded except it isn't much more than junk on wheels anyway. His girlfriend, Delilah—her silky skin the color of obsidian and her pixie-cut hair glimmering gold—sits unmoving in the back, apparently oblivious to it all. Me—I'm just trying to keep us all from dying.

Cheap beer has never sat well with me, and as we bounce madly across that backass desert road, it sloshes nauseatingly about in my belly. Add to that the sickly stream of fear coursing through my veins as we rip through the desert with the headlights off, and it's all I can do to keep from blowing chunks all over the dash.

Why are we out here in these godforsaken barrens on what seems like a suicide run? Well, that was Brandon's idea. Despite me clinging, white-knuckled, to the wheel in the driver's seat, I'm just along for the ride. I have always been the bookish type, believing truly and with full faith in that George R. axiom "A reader lives a thousand lives before he dies."

That being said, there is no substitute for the real deal, and Brandon is a genuine American lunatic if Nevada has ever borne one. Wherever he goes, whatever he does, as knuckle-brained as it may seem, I can be sure of one thing: it will be an experience. So I stick by his side. When he showed up at my door like some great monolith, with eyes dancing on the fringe, and fairly sang that it was time to get out of the city and lay waste to the Mojave, I went along.

We hit a particularly nasty dip in the road. For a moment, I'm sure that Brandon will go flying out the window, barreling into that dark wasteland, and a most unique monster will be lost to the world forever. I don't know if I would be saddened or relieved, but it's not to be. Instead, he drops back into his seat.

"Can we turn the blasted lights on now?" I ask.

Brandon turns in his seat to face me. He leans in until his nose is nearly touching mine. His eyes are wide and intense, and the veins in his massive neck stand out like great dunes. I think it a wonder that they don't burst and spew his lifeblood all about the innards of the van.

He says, "Death is the playground of all living things." Then he smiles and says, "Let us frolic."

And what can I say to that?

He turns away and grabs a beer from the cooler at his feet. He hands it to me, and I accept. He takes one for himself, pops the tab, throws his head back, and upends the can. The contents are gone in a matter of moments. He bellows mad laughter and chucks his dead soldier over his shoulder. The can smacks Delilah in the face.

"Stop," she says.

Brandon looks over to me, his brow sunken in concern. I slow the van to a stop and kill the engine. For a moment, we all sit in heavy silence. Delilah opens the door and steps out. We both follow suit. Outside the van, Brandon stands towering over Delilah. She says nothing but lashes out, her hand flying in an arc and raking him across the face. Blood wells up in three long lines across his cheek. She puckers her lips and spits. Her saliva splatters against his cheek, mingling with his blood.

Brandon looks at her with hurt shock.

"Penance," she says. She raises herself up and brushes her lips across his.

Brandon runs his fingers across the wound, then across his tongue.

"I'm sorry," he says.

"I know," she says and smiles.

He smiles back and asks, "Is it time?"

She looks about, seeming to consider, and finally says, "By all means."

Brandon retrieves something from the van. He turns to me and holds up a large plastic bag filled with what appears to be a mass of Cthulian pods.

A big smile spreads across his face.

"Peyote!"

-$-

I lie on the roof of the van, watching the stars form themselves into great curved pillars upon which the axis of the world rests. The desert expands and contracts in steady waves, as if taking deep and deliberate breaths. Beside me, Brandon and Delilah are coiled about each other, a writhing swirl of alabaster and obsidian.

I hear her whisper to him, "I will bear your children."

"A horde," he agrees.

I smile and tears roll down my face, for in that moment everything is poetry and beauty and sorrow and joy, and death is our playground, and we frolic like children. I stand and raise my arms out and try to embrace all things. I am swaying back and forth, a warm buzz tingling over my skull, when Delilah pops up like a rocket and screams, "Penny!" I startle and fall off the side of the roof.

I hit the ground, the breath knocked out of me. I lie looking up toward the sky, gasping, my lungs on fire. Overhead, Delilah's face pops up from above the van, like some celestial Kilroy.

"We need a penny," she says.

-$-

Delilah and I stand shoulder to shoulder, leaning against the hood of the van. Brandon is crouched on the roof, his knees spread wide and his fists resting upon the edge between them. The headlights are on, and we all look out across the road.

"What's going to happen?" I ask.

"I don't know," Delilah answers.

"When is it going to happen?"

"Soon."

"Is it going to be bad?"

Before she can answer, I catch a glimpse of a silhouette in the dark, just beyond the reach of the lights.

"Do you see that?" I ask.

"Yes."

"Is it a hallucination?"

"No."

"Should I be afraid?"

"Shh."

We watch in silence as the figure grows closer. Brandon's breath is loud and becomes increasingly agitated.

The man steps into the light. Brandon brings both fists down upon the roof over and over again, snarling like a wild animal caught in a trap. The man looks at each of us in turn, opens his mouth, and pulls something from beneath his tongue. He holds it up, clasped between index finger and thumb. The light glints off of it. He looks up at the beast upon the roof. He begins to speak and, though his lips move, I don't hear a thing. Instead, the words seep from between his teeth in great Lichtenstein bubbles. They waver in the air, and they read . . .

> "I bet you . . .
>> . . . a penny . . .
>>> . . . I can kick your ass."

. . . and they fall to the ground like lead.

The thing that is Brandon needs no further invitation. He leaps, clearing the hood, and hits the ground in a nuclear blast. The sound is deafening. The shock wave warps the landscape and brings me to my knees. As he hits, he explodes into an infinite line of Brandons that spread out to either horizon as far as I can see. They charge, a slipstream of flash frames echoing in their paths. They converge gradually at the speed of light upon the man who stands resolute, like a pillar to the gods. As they do, they grow until their brows scrape across the sky. Scales emerge across the entirety of their bodies, and great talons sprout from hands morphed into claws. They have, each of them, become Megabrandosaurus Rex. I behold this wall of irrefutable annihilation descending upon the man for an instantaneous eternity, and then the great beasts are upon him.

The man folds back into the earth, a real-life pop-up book in reverse, and as the beast passes over him, a foot comes up between its legs. The beast withers as it falls, and all its millions of copies dissolve into the sand until there is only Brandon, lying with his knees in his chest, his hands tucked between his legs. His head morphs into a spore, slick and bulbous and pulsating fitfully. The man stands over him and raises his heel. He brings it down, and the spore erupts, spraying the sky in a fine red mist.

He raises his heel to strike again, but Delilah is there, though she is Delilah no longer. She has become Ereshkigal, goddess of the underworld, and the dead grovel at her feet. She lays a hand upon the man's shoulder and turns him to face her.

"That's enough," she says. She becomes Lilith, that great seducer, with raven-black hair and a serpent coiled about her torso. She kisses him upon his brow.

He stares at her, stone faced and unmolested by her guile, and says, "My due."

She turns toward me. As she does, short black hair grows across her figure, and her eyes stretch and turn to emerald, and she is Bast. She points a claw toward me, and it reaches across the vast distance and plunges into my heart, and I cry out.

The man approaches and stands over me, his open hand extended. I place the single copper coin upon his palm. He steps over me, and I watch as he disappears down the road and into the desert night, heading toward the city proper.

I look back toward my companions, and for a moment, I see with clarity. Delilah kneels in the road, a shifting goddess no more. She holds Brandon cradled in her arms, tending to his wounds. He is hurt but intact. I roll onto my back and, looking up toward the heavens, I make a silent vow that I will never again indulge in hallucinogens.

-$-

The man walks along the road, his skin caked in a thin layer of dirt, blood, and cold sweat. Clenched in his fist are two copper coins. The young ones are miles behind. Alamo Road gives way to Moccasin Road, which ends abruptly at the corner of Log Cabin Way and North El Capitan. Packed dirt turns to black top, and street lamps light the way. Suburban homes stand like soldiers of conformity. The man marches down the road between them, nude and unkempt—an affront to all they hold dear.

-$-

Harold sits in the pale blue glow of *I Love Lucy* reruns. The couch bows beneath the nearly four hundred pounds of his frame. Deep purple patches sag beneath his eyes. Beside him is a cat—mangy, flea ridden, and sleeping in a cage. In his hand is a Mountain Dew. He drains the last remnants of the dull-yellow liquid and tosses the empty receptacle amongst the ever-growing pile of cans, discarded microwave dinner packages, and various candy wrappers that litter the floor.

He laughs uproariously at the black-and-white clichés that play across the screen, but the laughter is strained. He tries to bury the encroaching thoughts of his secret burden. His terrible responsibility is still vast minutes away. For now, he pretends to forget his solemn nightly duty and simply basks in the empty pleasure of the optical sedative before him.

He grabs another Mountain Dew, pops the tab, and gets to work on the eighth one of the night. It is a decision he will come to regret.

At precisely 2:00 a.m., just as the episode is wrapping up and the names of the dead begin to scroll across the backdrop of a faded gray heart, there is the audible click of a timer. The television shuts off, and the room is thrown into darkness. The blood drains from Harold's face, and his palms begin to sweat.

It is time. Even after all these years, he is still terrified to perform his duty. He supposes that it is a thing impossible to become accustomed to. But it is his charge, and so he rises, snatches up the cage of the sleeping feline, and wades through the debris of his hubris toward his room. Along the way, he picks up the Remington pump-action shotgun that leans against the wall.

Arriving at his room, Harold places an ear against the dilapidated wood of the closet door and finds nothing but silence. He kneels and pulls the cat from its cage. As he does, it awakens and lashes out, etching deep gashes into his arm. He pulls a syringe from his back pocket and slips the needle into its hide. Almost at once, the cat goes limp and its eyes swim in a drunken haze. He hopes it will help. He opens the closet door, tosses it inside, and slams the door shut. He waits. As he does, he tries to ignore the weak mewling of the feline inside.

Soon, the first stirrings of an unholy symphony begin inside the closet. There is the sound of insectile creatures scampering along plaster walls, the discordant wails of the forlorn, and the gnashing of teeth. The sounds of the countless horrors rise swiftly to a tumultuous pitch, the total summation of their discordant harmony a virulent proclamation— an anathema.

Weaving through this infernal cacophony, barely perceptible, is a singular voice. Its tone is sickly sweet, like some archaic lexicon that sings of a primal essence long forgotten. Harold does not grasp the exactness of the litany, but its meaning is clear. It longs for the taste of spilled bowels and torn flesh.

And so they have it in the form of the feline affectionately named Snack #6638. Its wretched howls are short but fierce as it is torn asunder. It is a paltry sacrifice to be sure, hopelessly inadequate to the task of satiating the hellish throng, but it is all he has to offer. He can only pray that it is enough.

Harold sits in the dark, crammed into the space between the dresser and the wall. His Remington is trained at the closet door on the far side of the room. Something slams against the door from within, rattling the frame, and his finger tightens on the trigger. Then it recedes, slow and heavy and wet. For a moment, all is silent, until the sounds of the countless horrors tentatively start back up. A low, guttural, rolling growl rumbles from within. Something foul sniffs loudly at the crack beneath the door. He fears that the offering did not suffice.

His joints ache and sweat stings his bloodshot eyes. His bladder is full to the point of bursting. He wants to relieve himself right then and there, but his momma always said, "It is a very bad thing to wet your pants. Little boys that wet their pants are carried straight off to hell."

Though momma never said just where that might be, Harold knows. Hell is just on the other side of that door. But by god, he has to go. He has to go right now! He has to go, or his bladder will burst and he will die and the things inside will get out. They would snatch him up, and they would drag him, dying and screaming, into the depths below, where he would be flayed and mauled and tortured by creatures unimaginable for all of eternity.

He sets the shotgun on the floor before him and, never taking his eyes off the door, places his hands against the dresser and the wall and laboriously heaves himself to his feet. The dresser rocks, and Herbie, his pet eucalyptus, falls to the floor. The pot does not shatter, but there is a loud thud. All the strange creatures within the closet cease their stirring. Harold stands rigid, his back against the wall. He holds his breath and stares intently at the closet door. Something seeps from the crack. It is thick, pink, and black with blisters and blood. It spreads across the floor like some kind of fleshy rug, raises, and seems to taste the air of the room for a presence. Finding nothing, it draws back and the sounds of the horrors slowly recommence. Harold lets out a breath of relief and snatches the shotgun from the floor.

He tiptoes his way to the window, wincing with each creak of the floorboards, and peaks out the blinds. Outside, all appears quiet and still. He raises the blinds and opens the window. He rests the shotgun against the sill, drops his trousers, and releases an arching yellow stream onto the front lawn. His relief is palpable but short lived. Standing with his back to the closet door, his flesh begins to crawl. The things inside can sense that his attention is momentarily diverted, and soon they will begin pouring out. He shakes off, zips up, and grabs his shotgun. He is about to turn when the pervert steps into the illumination of the street lamps like some divine gift from below.

Never before has he offered up a human sacrifice. But this is a pervert—an inhuman—surely deserving of the tribulations of hell. A quick decision is made, and Harold lugs himself over the windowsill, falling to the moist earth below. Rising, he lumbers across the yard with shotgun in hand.

-$-

The man puts up no resistance as he is herded through the window and into the room. Harold aims the shotgun at him. The closet behind the man shakes violently with the clamor of the damned, as if they can sense the feast to come. The man seems not to mind.

The man gestures to the shotgun. "Are you going to shoot me?"

"No, not unless I have to."

"Then why am I here?"

Harold reaches for the top of the dresser. His thick fingers fumble across the line of syringes lying there. He snatches one up and tosses it onto the floor in front of the man.

"Inject yourself," he says.

The man regards the syringe for a moment and asks, "Why?"

"It'll be better for you."

"How so?"

"You're going in there, one way or another," Harold says, gesturing toward the closet door. "And when you do, those things are going to do unspeakable things to you. There's a heavy sedative in that syringe. It will make it . . . better."

"And if I refuse?"

"Then I blow out your kneecaps, and you go in anyway. Without the sedative."

The man turns and places his hand upon the handle of the door.

"Wait! Stop!" Harold shouts, panic straining his voice.

The man stops and turns back to Harold.

"You'll let them out," Harold says.

"What is your name?" the man asks.

"Harold."

"Harold, I have a wager for you."

He holds out his fist and opens it revealing two copper coins.

"I will bet these talismans against your entire estate that I can rid you of your nightmares."

Harold squints at the coins in the man's palm incredulously.

"A couple of pennies?"

"Harold, you have no idea who or what I am. Watch."

The man holds out his hand with the coins in his palm and places his other hand on top. He closes his eyes and seems to concentrate. Then he removes his hand and produces the coins again.

"Do you see that?" he asks. "The way they glow?"

Harold did see.

"These are no ordinary tokens. They are talismans, and whosoever possesses them shall have dominion over the beasts of the night. Do you want them, Harold?"

Harold's mouth is dry, his eyes wide. He licks his lips and says, "I do."

"Then accept my wager."

"I accept."

The man nods and turns back to the closet door. He places his hand upon the handle, seemingly unconcerned by the hellish calamity beyond. He opens the door.

The horrors come flooding out, the shrieks of their bloodlust an epic orchestra of bedlam. Huge black tentacles, their surfaces slick and dripping viscous fluid, wrap about the man's limbs. Razor-sharp talons impale his chest. The withered hands of the countless damned grasp at his naked flesh. They rip him off the ground and drag him unceremoniously into the depths beyond. The door slams shut.

Cowering in his cranny between the dresser and the wall, Harold listens to the maelstrom of the feasting. There are shrieks and the crunching of bone. There is the wet sloshing and sucking of spilled entrails. There is the dry clicking of an ever-present death rattle. The sounds turn his stomach. After a time, the din dies down and all is silent. The man is dead. The creatures are fed. Harold breathes easy.

He is beginning to rise, ready to lay his tired bones to bed, when the door flies open. There stands the man. About him are all the armies of hell.

Harold screams as the legions of the abhorrent dead descend upon him. The man lied. There is no talisman to be had. He is Abaddon, the Beast, and ruler of them all. In an instant, the grim reality of his coming eternity passes through his mind. His reflexes are quick. The barrel of his shotgun rests beneath his chin.

There is an explosion, and a hole opens in the top of his head. What is left of Harold's thoughts drip languidly from the ceiling in thick red and gray chunks.

-$-

The man stands in the closet. It is empty, save for the pile of neighborhood pets upon which he stands. Their carcasses are in varying stages of decomposition, and the stench of their decay is thick. He looks toward his host. Harold swings the barrel of the shotgun up to rest under his chin. He pulls the trigger, and there is the sharp click of a dry fire. Harold throws his head back and collapses, his limbs splayed across the floor.

The man steps out of the closet, crosses the room, and kneels to inspect the catatonic, corpulent figure before him. Harold's eyes are blank, his jaw slack. A thin stream of spittle seeps from his mouth. Harold is relieved of his nightmare. The man stands, steps over the body, and exits the room.

Sometime later, the man steps out the front door, freshly showered and wearing a three-piece suit that fits like a deflated blimp. His hair is wet, his face clean. He holds in his hand a large bag and a set of keys. In the driveway is a 1983 Buick Riviera. He gets in, tosses the bag onto the seat beside him, and turns the ignition. It is reluctant at first, but he is soon cruising down the road toward the Las Vegas Strip.

-$-

The sun beats relentlessly down on the brow of the man as he walks amongst the crowds of the Las Vegas Strip. Sweat streams down his face and into his eyes. The car and the bag are gone, replaced by large wads of cash stuffed into the various pockets of his ill-fitting suit. He steps into the largest casino on the Strip and is greeted by cool air and the frantic clamor of slot machines, sirens, and roaring conversation.

Along one wall of the entrance is a line of photographs. The man walks to the wall. He looks up at a photograph that is larger than and hangs above all the rest. Displayed within the boisterously elegant, golden frame is an older man with balding black hair and a smile that fails to reach his eyes. Beneath the photograph is a little gold plaque. It reads:

Martin Mathews
Owner/CEO of Bagetta Hotels and Casinos

-$-

The man sits beneath the shade of the tree, watching the house from across the street. The habitat is a monument to decadence, a garish behemoth secured behind a tall wrought-iron fence.

He sits there watching for long hours until the sun goes down and the lights go out. He climbs over the fence, slinks across the wide plain of green grass, and slips in through the bathroom window.

-$-

I wake to the sound of an unfamiliar voice whispering in my ear. It is saying, "Up and to the left."

If more terrifying words have ever been muttered, I've never heard them. I fling my eyes open, but all I catch is a dark blur before something long, cold, and hard presses against the underside of my chin. It forces my head up and to the left. There is the sharp prick of a needle sinking into my neck, and I plummet into a dreamless void.

When I wake again, I find myself tied to a chair in my room. My vision is swimming, and I am encased in a full-body cast of Novocain. Some slimy fucker is sitting across from me, all casual with a shotgun laid across his lap.

The clothes he wears must be five times his size, and they drape over the sides of the chair like curtains. It would be comical on any other man in the world, but this guy, hell . . .

Listen, have you ever heard the phrase *mad as a hatter?* Well, think of the polar opposite. Think of the opposite of feral, the yang of delirium. Think of a deep, composed sanity that is nearly otherworldly. That is this man in spades. I read people; it's what I do. I'm a gambler by nature—a businessman. But I won both those games long ago, and I'm bored. So when this man says "I'm here to offer you a wager, Mr. Mathews"—well fuck me, how can I not accept?

The man nods to a pile of cash on the floor before him and says, "I'll flip you for it."

There can't be more than twenty grand there. Imagine my disappointment. This sorry sack of shit creeps into my room in the dead of night and pumps my veins full of god knows what, and for what? Some pathetic pile of greasy cash.

So I tell this tosser, "If you're looking to gamble some petty cash, you can head on down to one of my casinos."

He says, "Your casinos are rigged. I'm looking for a straight game. Fifty-fifty odds."

So I explain to him, "That quarter, the one everyone's carrying around in their pockets and flipping when they run into some stupid decision they're too incompetent to make—like whether to have the mushroom cheeseburger or the pot roast—that coin is weighted on the side of Washington's big fat head." I tell this man, "There is only one fair game on God's green earth."

I say, "If you've come here, to me, then you're after more than some little pile of cash. If that's not the case, then fuck you; you might as well blow me away right now. But if you want to play a game—a game with some actual stakes—well then, you have my attention."

"What is your game, Mr. Mathews?" he asks.

"Cut me free, and we can speak more," I say.

"Are you a man of your word?"

"Above all things."

"And your game is fair?"

"Absolutely equitable."

And to my amazement, this guy lays down his gun, stands, walks around behind me, and looses my bonds.

I stand, and my legs are uneasy. I'm still woozy from the drugs. He grabs my elbow, steadying me.

I wave him away and say, "I can stand on my own."

I stumble to my bedside table and pick up the phone. He gives me a look, but I tell him, "Don't worry. As I said, I am a man of my word." I say into the receiver, "Get security up here."

I hang up, and I say to this man, "I have three possessions that I prize above all other things. That is the first of them." I indicate the painting above my bed. "And it will tell you two very important things about me."

He looks, but he does not speak.

Above the bed is a painting of two men locked in combat. One stands behind the other, his knee shoved into the other's back, forcing it into a painful arch. His teeth are buried in his rival's throat. Below them is a man fallen. Behind the combatants, two men watch in quiet contemplation. In the distance is a demon, its arms crossed, observing the onlookers with unconcealed contempt.

"This is a painting of Dante and Virgil in the eighth circle of hell. It was painted by William Bouguereau in 1850," I say. "It is believed to be currently hanging in the Musée d'Orsay in Paris. It is not. The one at the Musée is a fake. What you are currently looking at is the original. It is priceless, both monetarily and existentially. It is a work of unsurpassed beauty; do you not agree?"

"And what is this supposed to tell me about you?" the man asks.

"It tells you that I can get anything on this earth that I want. It tells you that I have what you are after, and if I don't, I can get it."

"And the second thing it's supposed to tell me?" he asks.

Just then, there is a knock on the door.

"Come in!" I yell.

Two men, both in black, step into the room. Their weapons are drawn. Their eyes light up with surprise when they see the man with me.

I ask them, "Who's monitoring the cameras?"

"Geoffery," one of them replies.

"He's fired. Have someone tune him up and get him out of here."

I turn back to the man and say, "These men will escort you to your quarters."

-§-

The next night, my men follow me down to the sublevels of my home, to my special little room. It is dark, and the smell of the room is musky with old sweat and damp wood. The man sits quietly in the corner of his cell. When I ask if his quarters are suitable, he doesn't say a thing. I remove my clothing, and my men strap cuffs about my wrists and string me up to the hook screwed into the wooden plank overhead. He observes through the bars but remains silent.

He does not call out when my men begin to beat me. A fist smashes into my face, and my lip splits, spilling blood into my mouth and down my chin. A knee connects with my ribs, and I groan. Sticks of wood beat across my body, leaving large welts and bruises in their wake.

81

When they are done with their work, they release me, and I fall—bloody, beaten, and broken—to the floor.

They leave, and I drag myself to my feet and begin to dress. As I do, I say to the man, "I have had everything this world can provide. I have had women and men. I have experienced every thrill I can imagine. I have had every drug man has known: marijuana, amphetamines, LSD, ecstasy, heroin, crack, and cocaine. Their highs were exquisite. But let me tell you something I learned. The suffocating pain of detox and withdrawal was more so."

I step to the cell, wrap my hands about the bars, and stare into his eyes.

"You see, to experience is to be alive. Pleasure is such an overrated sensation. Pain, loss, agony—these emotions, these experiences, are so much more raw, so much more powerful. When you are swept up in the tides and drowning in the maelstrom of a great personal anguish—this is when you are truly alive. Sensations of pleasure pale in comparison." I say, "I would like to offer you the opportunity to live. Are you ready to discuss the terms of our wager?"

The man just nods.

As we climb the stairs to the top level of my home, I tell him, "When I was a boy, a few weeks before Christmas, my dog went missing. I loved that dog. My brother consoled me. I think he genuinely felt bad for me. He seemed truly distraught. Come Christmas morning, he woke me and said that Santa had left me a very special present. I, of course, didn't care. I was inconsolable. He was insistent, and he took my hand and dragged me down the stairs and to the Christmas tree. He pointed to one of the packages. The wrapping—it had little Christmas elves sitting at benches making toys. I took it and opened it, and do you want to know what was inside? It was my dog. It still had nails plunged into its eyes. Its ribs were sticking out of its side. Two of its legs were missing. You see, he had taken my dog, and he had tortured it for weeks before it finally died."

We reach the top of the stairs and come to a door of deep rosewood inlaid with intricate gold lacework. I open the door, and we step inside. In the center of the room is a pedestal. The walls are lined with shelves of mahogany. Upon these shelves, in little rows, are jars filled with a sepia fluid. Each jar is adorned with its own little golden placard.

One of the jars says:

Dillon Bixby
January 8th 1986
Treachery

Another says:

Devin Thoreau
September 17th 1993
Disloyalty

I say to him, "So, do you know what I did? I beat him. I beat him until he was bloody and unconscious. Our parents slept through the whole thing."

I walk to a shelf, the centermost one in the room, and I pull one jar down. I say, "I dragged him into our mother's sewing room. I tied him up—much the same way you tied me up."

I carry the jar across the room, caressing it along the way. I place it in the man's hands, and I say, "I gagged him, grabbed a pair of scissors, and cut off his balls."

Floating in the jar are two white and shriveled pods.

"My parents woke to his screams and ran down, and I ran away. I hid in my bed, pretending to be asleep. They found him like that, with his balls on the sewing room floor amongst a pool of blood and a pair of scissors lying beside them."

The placard on the jar reads:

David Monroe Mathews
December 25th 1970
Murder

"This was the first of my collection. My second most-prized possession. And that," I say, indicating the scissors that lie upon the pedestal, "is the tool I used to acquire them. That is my wager to you. The only wager I am willing to accept. So, do you?" I ask.

"I do," the man says.

-$-

We are heading toward the bottom-most level of my home. My guards follow along beside us. I'm saying to the man, "You know, my brother—he never did say what happened to him. The doctors assumed he did it to himself. They ran tests, MRIs, brain scans—that kind of thing. They determined he was a psychopath, though they never could figure why he did that to himself. Unusual behavior for his kind and all that."

"What is the game?" the man asks.

"Ah, yes, the game," I say. "There is only one game in the entirety of existence that is fair. It is fair by the very nature of reality. Men and women both play this game. The birds and the insects and the fish and all the viruses in the world play it. Hell, even the celestial bodies of the stars and planets and black holes play this game. In men, it is determined by genetics, by will, by upbringing, by discipline, and by chance. All of the choices that a man has made in his life ultimately bring him to the culmination of the game. And in this game, there are no rules."

We come to a set of large oak doors. The chaotic ruckus from the other side drifts, softly muffled, through the wood.

I say, " 'They smote each other not alone with hands, but with the head and with the breast and feet, tearing each other piecemeal with their teeth.' " I turn to him. "It's a quote, you see. From Dante Alighieri's Divine Comedy. It's the passage for which my painting is depicted."

I swing the doors wide. Inside, the room is filled with packed dirt. The dirt is warm with the stamping feet of the throngs. They shout and yell and spit around a large, white circle drawn on the ground.

"I host these events once a month," I say to him. "Your time of arrival was quite fortuitous."

In the center of the circle, two men writhe in battle, one on top of the other.

"You would not believe how much people will gamble on the lives of others," I say.

The man on top digs his thumbs into his victim's eyes, and a scream of agony tears across the chants of the crowd. He dips his head down, and his teeth sink into the soft pink flesh of the man's cheek. He comes back up with it hanging from between his teeth. He chews and swallows as his victim cries and flails to no effect. The man on top does this over and over again, until what's left of his victim's face isn't much more than a mass of blood and protruding bone. He does this until I shout above the crowd, "Enough!" He rises and smiles with blood streaming down his chin and across his chest.

I turn to the man and say, "My third, and most valued, possession: my brother." I say, "You're next."

-$-

The man stands inside the circle with the mad cannibal across from him. The crowd chants in frantic unison around them. The throng pump their arms and legs in strong, aggressive rhythms. The mad cannibal dances with them. His eyes—locked on the eyes of the man. His face—red with blood and strain.

They all chant in unison. They chant, "*Ka mate! Ka mate!*"

They all chant and dance the Haka. It is a terrifying and glorious sight that ends in the climax of a primal bloodlust howl.

I shout, "Fight!"

My brother rushes the man. The man turns and runs. He runs straight at me. My guards do their job and form a barrier around me, and the man collides into them. It's a domino effect, and we all go tumbling over. The crowd is still shouting. I'm lying flat on my back, buried beneath a metric shit-ton of useless meatheads, but I can still see when the man jumps to his feet. For a moment, everything plays out in slow motion. My brother is hanging in the air, midlunge, a breath away from tearing the man asunder. The man stands rigid, his arm held out in a straight line. Something in his fist gleams with reflected light, and I know immediately what it is. It is the gun from one of my guards' holsters. There is an explosion of sound. A hole opens in my brother's chest. Everything resumes its natural speed, and my brother is slammed to the ground by the force of the bullet. He clutches at his chest, his eyes wide in disbelief. The man walks casually to him, points the barrel at his head, and blows his brains out across the arena floor.

I scramble to my feet. My men do the same. Their weapons are trained upon the man.

I shout, "You shot him!" I can barely hear my own words.

He says, "There were no rules. Are you man of your word, Mr. Mathews?"

My face drains of color, and my knees go weak.

-$-

We are standing in the little round room with the jars. Between us is the pedestal. Atop the pedestal are the large, silver scissors. My pants lie bunched around my ankles. The man reaches down and takes the scissors. He holds them up, and the light of the room reflects softly across their sharp, polished edge. He steps around the pedestal and falls to his knees before me. He opens the scissors wide, and I feel the cold steel slide across the sack just above my balls. This is my great moment of loss, my great moment of personal anguish. My heart is pounding and my head swims. A sickening wave of nausea rolls over me, and I shout, "Stop! I can't do it."

He stops, looks up at me, and says, "This is when you are truly alive."

He begins to squeeze the scissors closed. A single bead of blood slides along their edge.

I scream, "There must be something else!"

He stops again and looks up at me and says, "Everything."

I shout at him, "Do you have any idea what I'm worth?"

The scissors begin to close again, and the blood really begins to flow.

"All right!" I scream. "All right! Everything!"

He stops again and looks up into my eyes. He says, "Are you a man of your word, Mr. Mathews?"

I bow my head, and I say, "Above all things."

The last time I see him, he is walking down my drive with a suitcase in one hand. He said he would give me a week to get my affairs in order but that he needed this one thing straightaway. He never does come back for the rest.

-$-

It is Saturday night, two minutes from Sunday morning. The man stands in the desert, looking out across the dark and barren road. A suitcase rests at his feet. In the distance, a black limousine approaches.

-$-

Seven Days Earlier

The man—his name is Alden Hudson—kneels on the grass in his front lawn. His knees are wet with early-morning dew. Tears run down his face. Behind him, his home is engulfed in a roaring inferno. His neighbors don't seem to notice or care. In front of him, a small oriental man, with a slick, greasy black bowl cut and large white teeth, sits smiling in a lawn chair. His wife is propped up in a sitting position on the ground between the little man's knees. The top half of her skull is missing, and her brain lies exposed. It's all mashed up into large chunks. The oriental man dips his hand in and squeezes, and when he pulls it back out, it looks as if it's covered in mashed potatoes intermixed with red meat. Running the flat of his palm across his tongue, he grimaces. He says to the man, "Honestly, I have no idea what you saw in her. This is disgusting."

Alden Hudson screams in impotent rage.

Next to the oriental man's feet are Alden's daughters. Twins with blonde hair and pale-blue eyes. They are asleep, their gentle snores uninterrupted by the chaos around them.

The oriental man nudges his wife's body, and it falls over lifelessly. The soup of her brains spills across the lawn. The oriental man stands and snatches up the twins, one in each arm. Alden tries to rise, to stop this fiend, to murder him, to rip him limb from limb, but the little oriental man turns and wags his finger.

He says, "Na, ah, ah, Mr. Hudson. That is no way to treat a guest."

Then Alden falls to the ground in violent convulsions. He foams at the mouth. His muscles expand and contract in agonizing spasms. Through the seizure, Alden can only watch as the oriental man dumps his daughters into the trunk of the black limousine, shuts the lid, and returns.

Standing over him, the fiend says, "If I make that stop, will you play nice?" He kneels down in the grass, his knees inches from the man's bouncing head, and he says, "Your daughters—they can sleep through this whole thing, or they can be awake through it. The choice is yours, Alden. So, what's it going to be?"

The only thing that comes out of his mouth is a spasmodic series of grunts.

"I'll take that as a yes," he says. Instantly, the convulsions cease.

Alden jumps to his feet. He snatches the oriental man up by the throat. He drags him into the street. He slams him down and beats his head into the curb. Alden screams as he does this, spittle flying from his lips. He kicks the oriental man's head into the curb until he falls, exhausted and crying, in the street.

And the oriental man sits up, his face a bloody pulp. He says, "Well, if that's the way you're going to be."

He snaps his fingers, and a pounding begins from the trunk of the limousine. Alden can hear his daughters crying for him, and he cries back.

The oriental man sits cross-legged in the street and says, "I want to offer you a wager."

He says, "I'm going to drop you off in Las Vegas. If you can bring me back a million dollars, then you can have your daughters back. But there are a few rules. No stealing. No cheating. You go in with nothing . . . save this." He holds up a single copper penny.

He says, "Open wide," and he places the coin beneath Alden's tongue.

"You have seven days."

He taps Alden's watch and says, "You can keep that."

"Why are you doing this?" Alden asks.

The oriental man shrugs and says, "Oh, I'm bored, and I'm waiting on someone."

-$-

The stars slip like diamonds across the black mirror surface of the limousine as it arrives. It pulls up to park before him, and the engine cuts off. The front door opens, and the little oriental man steps out. His face is smooth, unblemished by any sign of assault. He walks around to the back with a smile on his face, and he lifts the lid of the trunk. Inside are Alden's two little girls. They sit side by side, motionless, their faces placid, staring into each other's eyes. They do not cry, and they do not call for him.

"What did you do to them?" Alden asks. His voice is hoarse and cracks with heartache.

"Oh, no one has touched them, I assure you."

"Then what's wrong with them?"

"I had to go out. I had things to do. I didn't have anywhere to keep them, so I left them at home. They've . . . they've seen some things." The oriental man laughs. He slaps Alden on the shoulder as if they were long-time buds and says, "The things they've seen, you would not even believe!"

"I will kill you."

"No, you won't." The little man taps the suitcase with his foot and asks, "Is that my million dollars?"

"It is."

"Show it to me."

Alden kneels down, lays the case on its side, and pops the latch. The lid flings open, revealing neat stacks of green cash.

"Now give me my daughters."

A smile spreads across the fiend's face, and he says, "I knew you had it in you. I just knew it. I am so proud of you." The smile drops away, and he adds, "Or I would be if you didn't renege by breaking the rules."

"I didn't break the rules."

"There were four rules. Just four!" he screams. "Do you not remember what they were?"

"No cheating. No stealing. I go in with nothing. I have seven days."

"And you broke the second rule. You stole!"

"I stole nothing!" Alden shouts.

"You stole a gun from a security guard in order to murder a hapless cannibal."

Alden struggles to compose himself. "I didn't steal; I borrowed."

The oriental man turns and walks back to the car. He picks up one of the girls and carries her back to him. Alden takes his daughter in his arms and holds her tight. She does not hug back, and her eyes never leave the eyes of her sister.

The oriental man says, "We'll call it halfsies, then, all right? You sort of fulfilled your end of the bargain, so I'll sort of fulfill mine."

"I'm not leaving here without both of my daughters."

"Then another wager?"

Alden's shoulders drop as he asks, "What is your wager?"

"I will give you the other daughter if you can eat that million dollars before sunrise."

Alden sets his daughter down beside him. He falls to his knees before the suitcase and begins shoving hundred dollar bills into his mouth as tears stream from his eyes.

# ABOUT THE COVER ARTIST

**Verstandt R. A. Shelton** is Inklings Publishing's cover artist. Growing up as a childhood misfit, Verstandt R. A. Shelton wiled away the hours daydreaming of floating in space and sitting at the bottom of the ocean floor. A disquieting obsession for the less beaten paths of philosophical ponderings and environmental extremes led him to stumble into the murky depths of the writerly craft. You can find him today chained in the back of his closet with the lights out, a bottle of whiskey in hand, and the ghosts of his inspirations (Stephen King, Clive Barker, Milton, Lovecraft, and Dante) breathing down his neck, writing stories to terrify the world. His lovely wife, Jennifer, and his cat, Siouxsie Q, worry for his safety.

# ABOUT THE AUTHORS

**Emerson Adair** is a Texas resident who loves stories. Sharing tales, whether they spring from real experiences or flights of fancy, is a passion developed from early childhood, when her father read her fairy tales by the fireplace. She worked for seven years at a small-town newspaper in the Coastal Bend area and now works to promote higher education.

**Melissa Algood** was born in California and is a proud Navy brat who has moved over twenty times in her life, although Stafford, Texas, has become her home. She contributed to her college newspaper and literary magazine as not only a staff writer but an editor. With a passion for the dark and eerie in all of her writings, she hopes to keep her audience enthralled with her characters' lives, especially in her previously published work *Blood on the Potomac*. Melissa works as a hairstylist, and she finds a lot of inspiration from the thousands of clients she's met over the course of her career (although none of them have actually admitted to being a serial killer). She enjoys playing her guitar, reading, watching TV shows with strong antiheroes, and collecting anything related to Harry Potter.

**Andrea Barbosa** is the author of *Massive Black Hole*, *Olympian Passion*, and *Holes in Space*. She has a bachelor's degree in tourism. She took creative writing courses at Texas Tech University. She loves to travel, read, and write poetry and fiction. She maintains an indie review blog and was a contributor on *Yahoo Contributor Network* and *Yahoo! Voices* websites. Her work has been influenced by Joyce Carol Oates, Erica Jong, Sylvia Plath, and contemporary Brazilian authors Paulo Coelho and Fernando Sabino, among others. Currently, she serves as author events director for the Houston Writers Guild.

**Gwen Hart** teaches writing at Buena Vista University in Storm Lake, Iowa. Her poems and stories have appeared in journals and anthologies, such as *MARGIE*, *Calliope*, *Lake Effect*, and *Measure*. Her poetry collection, *Lost and Found*, is available from David Robert Books.

**Christina Morales** has a BA in psychology from the University of Houston, has worked over a decade volunteering for social causes, and regularly publishes in Image Magazine of Brazoria County. She visits Vegas once a year for the peacefulness she finds there.

**Daniel O'Connor** was born the youngest of five children, in Brooklyn, New York. He lost his mother to cancer, on her wedding anniversary, when he was four years of age and then his father, two years later. He fought his way through life, eventually becoming a decorated New York police officer. He now lives in the Southwest with his wife and daughters. His thriller novel, *Sons of the Pope*, has been optioned for television, and he has suspense stories in *Blood Rites* and *Serial Killer Iterum*. His blog has been read by over one million people in more than two hundred countries and excerpted by the *NY Daily News*, *Washington Post*, *BuzzFeed*, and many other news agencies. He is currently working on his second novel.

**Caroline Sposto** has been published in *The Saturday Evening Post*, *Family Circle Magazine*, and an assortment of literary magazines and anthologies in the US, the UK, and Canada. In 2011, she was chosen to participate in the Moss Workshop in Fiction at the University of Memphis with author Richard Bausch. In 2013, she won second place in *The Great American Think-off*, an amateur philosophy competition that culminates in a public debate in New York Mills, Minnesota.

**Verstandt R. A. Shelton** is Inklings Publishing's cover artist. Growing up as a childhood misfit, Verstandt R. A. Shelton wiled away the hours daydreaming of floating in space and sitting at the bottom of the ocean floor. A disquieting obsession for the less beaten paths of philosophical ponderings and environmental extremes led him to stumble into the murky depths of the writerly craft. You can find him today chained in the back of his closet with the lights out, a bottle of whiskey in hand, and the ghosts of his inspirations (Stephen King, Clive Barker, Milton, Lovecraft, and Dante) breathing down his neck, writing stories to terrify the world. His lovely wife, Jennifer, and his cat, Siouxsie Q, worry for his safety.

Sneak Peek
# Mr. Landen's Library
by
**Fern Brady**

Enjoy the first three episodes
of this exciting blog series
from Inklings Publishing author
Fern Brady.
This blog will be presented in episodes
of exactly one thousand words each
—no more, no less.

# Mr. Landen's Library
*Fern Brady*

## Episode 1: Clara

"Don't touch the book!"

"Bitch," Clara mumbled, withdrawing her hand from the green leather-bound volume on the circulation desk.

"I heard that!" Esmeralda yanked up the book, sashaying to the special collections room at the back of the library.

Clara meandered to the cozy nook by the bay window and plopped herself onto one of the velvet couches. Pulling out her iPod, she sank into the plush cushion and closed her eyes.

The pressure of Mr. Landen's hand on her shoulder, startled Clara. She paused the song in time only to catch the old man's final words. " . . . doing homework."

"Yes, sir," She feigned meekness. "I have a science project coming up on local plants. Do you have anything I can read for that?"

Mr. Landen hesitated, rubbing bony fingers on his chin. "Well . . . there is a very good book in the special collection." His eyes locked with hers. She willed herself to exude innocence. "These books are very valuable. You must use extreme care when handling them."

He turned, motioning her to follow him. Passing by where Esmeralda was shelving books, Clara stuck her tongue out at the fat bully, smiling broadly when she saw the look of disgust, then envy, in the woman's green eyes.

~

"I haven't finished and I'll be allowed back in school tomorrow. May I take it home? I'll bring it back really early in the morning."

She had sat in the closed off room all day listening to music, never even cracking the book open. Away from Esmeralda's hateful gaze, Clara had enjoyed, as much as possible, her incarceration in this stupid library.

"Clara, if you are going to take it with you, then I will need you to promise to follow the rules I'm about to set." The seriousness on Mr. Landen's wrinkled face gave Clara a tinge of guilt. Her prude teachers were going to fail her anyway, so why bother doing the work. But she liked the idea of walking out, special book in hand, past Esmeralda.

"I promise. I'll do everything just as you ask."

~

She opened her eyes, aware that she had been asleep. Clara felt heavy, as if she were held down by strong ropes that tightened deliberately. Something squeezed on her midsection causing a dull ache.

Looking about her, she noticed strange, curling vines with long broad leaves taking over her room. She tried to rise from the bed, only to realize that she was utterly bound, secured there, face up, arms pinned to her sides, legs splayed out.

They were everywhere. They were spreading.

Clara wondered where the climbers had come from. She owned no live greenery. Then she saw it – the book open on her nightstand. A gray-green mist danced with fluid serpentine motions over its pages.

Mr. Landen's warning rang in her head. 'Don't ever leave this book open after midnight.' What could possibly happen? She asked herself derisively. Out loud she had vowed to heed his words.

But Clara was not known for her obedience. Her constant refusal to follow the teacher's instructions at school was the reason she had been at the antiquated little lending library in the first place. Her single-parent mom usually relied on Mr. Landen's kindness when Clara got herself suspended.

Now, as she lay there almost entirely immobilized by the lush verdant sprouts that kept on growing and curling themselves around her bed, the teen remembered that the book was about local flora. *Surely, the creepers had not come from the book, had they?* Turning her head slightly, the bright green neon of her alarm clock told her it was one-fifteen in the morning.

She tried again in vain to break free of her assailant's tenacious grip, but to no avail. She raised her head to call to her mother, sleeping soundly next door. As her mouth opened, a shoot rose before her, spreading hood-like leaves that mimicked a cobra's cowl. Clara jerked her arms frantically hoping to shield herself from the looming attacker. Her efforts proved futile. Swiftly, it thrust into her mouth and spiraled through her throat muffling her call. It began to pool in her stomach stretching her abdomen.

Clara gagged. Vomit rose up her esophagus, but was pushed back down by the entering plant.

Fear gripped her. Her heart thumped wildly. She could hardly breathe. The vine continued its invasion, filling her ever more. Her pink lace cami gave way to the sight of the grotesque balloon of distended skin, elevating her increasing sense of horror.

She thrashed about, desperate to free herself from the insidious enemy. The pressure of the constriction from within grew taut. Warm wetness issued unbidden from between her legs. Urine squirted out as the enlarging gut crushed her bladder.

Exhausted after but a brief momentary struggle, she stilled.

Closing her eyes, Clara forced herself to calm down. Why had she left the book open on purpose? He'd warned her! She had thought him daft, addled. Who cared at what hour a book was open or closed? She had done the opposite just because; now she regretted not doing as she was told.

Regaining her determination, she chomped down on the straw size stem between her teeth, shoving the invader from her mouth with her tongue.

A small tickle made her sneeze, opening her eyes. Two strands of vine were positioned at each nostril. 'No!' she screamed in her head, her eyes grew wild with renewed panic. Curling sinuously, the plant rushed in.

A burst of pain rolled through her body, as the shoot punctured her lung, wrapping itself around the vital organ. With vice-like strength the vine contracted. Her fate was now sealed!

Clara could do nothing but await her end. She could no longer draw breath. Her body convulsed violently as the last of her oxygen was depleted. Her heart beat dropped. Her eyes dilated and widened, her muscles went limp. As her brain died, Clara's last fleeting thought was that she should have followed Mr. Landen's instructions.

## Episode 2: Esmeralda

Esmeralda awoke from another sweltering night of hot flashes and sweaty sheets. Menopause was upon her with a vengeance. No matter the A/C's setting, her own body's heat meant marinating in her own juices. Her red hair stuck to her head as if glued there. The oversized white camisole that reached down to her knobby knees, practically see-through from the night's sweating, clung to her plump form.

Rising disgusted, she trudged over to the miniscule bathroom of her single-room studio for a refreshing shower. The cool water did nothing to relieve the ever-simmering anger at the unfairness of her life.

~

Arriving at work, Esmeralda prepared for another boring day at Mr. Landen's Library. This small business, which stayed afloat by selling memberships, had taken Esmeralda in when no one else would. Although no charges had been filed, the stigma of the missing money from Elgar, Davilos, and Dunn, the accounting firm she had been happily employed with for over 15 years, had made her persona non grata. Of course Esmeralda knew it had been Mr. Davilos' son, Tony, who had taken the funds during his internship the previous summer. Of course, she had no proof. Of course, it was her accounts that had money missing – the little shit had disliked her from the start.

Esmeralda knew she should be grateful. Old Landen trusted her with the lending library's bookkeeping. But Esmeralda resented the work. For a CPA of her caliber, to go from managing million dollar accounts to these meager columns was demeaning. How this place stayed afloat was beyond her!

Settling at the circulation desk, Esmeralda hoped Clara didn't get herself suspended again. Playing babysitter for that brat was adding insult to injury. Reaching for one of the heavy tomes Mr. Tanner had returned that morning, she grunted at the musty smell of the older volume's yellowing pages.

The silver bell over the door announced Mr. Landen's arrival. One look at his haggard face sent a chill down Esmeralda's spine.

"Clara is dead," he announced without preamble.

"How?"

For a moment their eyes met. The old man's blue eyes seemed haunted.

"Suffocation. The police found . . . "

Silence blanketed the elegantly appointed rooms.

Exasperated by the drama, Esmeralda spat out, "What? What did they find?"

"A leaf." Mr. Landen clutched the book Clara had taken home yesterday to his chest.

The gold lettering stood out against the forest green leather of its binding. With solemnity, Mr. Landen strode to the private section located in the back. Only a handful of members were allowed in that room. Esmeralda was kept out, but Clara had gained access, that little monster.

~

The day dragged on. No other members visited. Mr. Landen remained in his office. Esmeralda passed the time posting her disgruntled thoughts on Facebook. Fifteen minutes before the official time she was supposed to go, Esmeralda slid out of her seat. Grabbing her things, she headed to the door, her gypsy-style skirt swaying with the movement of her wide hips.

Mr. Landen's voice halted her escape. "You live near Mrs. Waterson, don't you?"

"Yeees." Oh God! Esmeralda knew he would ask her to drop off a book. She hated being courier.

"Deliver this volume to her, please."

"Sure." Esmeralda yanked it from his outstretched hands, stuffing it into her oversized canvas bag.

"Esmeralda, make sure you take it straight to her. It's from the special collection!" his voice cut-off as the door slammed shut.

~

Whatever! Mrs. Waterson, a block over, could wait. She'd take the woman the stupid book after dinner. If the old fart wanted speedy service he should have hired the local bike couriers. She was a professional, for Pete's sake!

Tossing her bag in a corner, Esmeralda busied herself in the kitchenette. Soon she settled in front of her small TV to watch Survivor. The tome and Mrs. Waterson forgotten.

~

Esmeralda felt a sudden sharp pain on her ankle. She opened her eyes. Looking at the cable box's clock she realized it was well after midnight.

Must have fallen asleep, she thought to herself, stretching the kinks from her neck.

Tiny claws scurried over her bare feet. With a gasp, she jumped up onto her chair. The unfortunate piece of furniture groaned from and nearly toppled over.

Gazing about the space, Esmeralda realized she was surrounded by rats. Large, sharp-toothed, pink-tailed rodents skittered about on every surface of her tiny apartment.

They were multiplying.

More of them sprang from the corner of the room. The old volume Mr. Landen had entrusted to her lay open. Rats materialized from the strange gray-green mist that hovered over its pages.

She had to get out of here! But how? The path to the door seethed with rodents, their brown and gray fur matted with blood from gnawing and feeding on each other.

"Help! Somebody!" Esmeralda hollered.

The rats froze. All heads turned. Glowing yellow eyes fixed on her, balanced precariously upon the hapless recliner.

A stillness gripped the previously crawling mound of rodents. Then, as if on a telepathic cue, they plunged toward her. Swarming and pushing, they clawed their way up. The old frayed cloth shredding from their weight. Soon, however, their persistence paid off.

The lounger fell over.

Esmeralda lay on a cushion of wriggling rats. For a moment nothing happened. Then sharp fangs tore chunks off her fleshy legs and razor claws ripped at her clothing.

She let out an ear-piercing scream. Rats scuttled into her mouth, shoving their way down her throat in single file lines of almost military precision. Others nibbled at the edges of her mouth, her lips, and her tongue.

In excruciating agony, Esmeralda thrashed wildly, fighting in futility to make a run for the door. But the massive bulk of the ever-multiplying rodents held her firmly trapped.

Esmeralda twitched as the rats made a feast of her plump person, both inside and out. Her last thought was that she should have told the old geezer to take the damn book himself.

## Episode 3: Charles

Mr. Landen sat in the sofa by the picture window, gazing at the park across the street from his library. He breathed in the smell of musky old books, bound in leather, mustering up his courage. Clearly, he had been a poor keeper. Detective James Halloway was beginning to connect the dots; albeit, they made no sense to him.

"This book is from your library," Halloway had stated only an hour ago.

"Yes. Esmeralda delivered was to take it to Mrs. Waterson. How is it you have it, Detective?"

"Esmeralda died last night. She was . . . eaten . . . by some animal in her apartment." The detective's eyes stared steadily into Landen's own.

"What! My God! How . . . This is so . . . " Mr. Landen shook his head with very real sadness. Why hadn't the over-proud woman just delivered the book?

"Clara spent a lot of time here recently, I'm told." Halloway was fishing for information. "Seems strange two deaths and somehow connected to you."

Landen gave Halloway a stern gaze. "Are you saying I might have caused their deaths?"

An awkward silence fell on them.

"Of course not," the Detective dismissed the notion. "Well, best get back to the station. Have a good day."

Now, Landen shook his head, knowing full well Halloway was correct. It was his books, not himself, who'd committed the murderers.

A heart-weary sigh escaped his lips as he realized destroying the library was the best way to ensure these things did not continue. True, most of his patrons for special collections knew the risks and took the precautions seriously. But Mr. Landen was just not cut out for this kind of burden. There had been no mistakes for so long, he had begun to believe it would all be alright. And then it started again.

He looked down at the portrait of his beautiful wife. Her dark black hair and emerald green eyes beamed up at him. "We'll be together again soon, my love," he brought the frame to his lips, then reverently placed it on the round mahogany table beside his chair.

Standing he turned and faced the tomes sitting so harmlessly on the great oak bookcases. He had doused the place with gasoline when he had arrived back from picking up all the volumes currently checked out. Now, he struck the match; the flame bursting to life.

"I'm sorry. I just can't handle this." He dropped the match.

The blaze roared to life. The heat of the fire, fueled by the combustible liquid, seared through his clothing. His flesh began to burn. His screams echoed in the stillness of the room. He crumbled to the floor and rolled back and forth. He was on the verge of losing consciousness when he heard a loud 'whoosh'. Glitter-colored dust spread through the library, extinguishing the conflagration, except around him.

~

Mr. Charles Landen pulled into a nice spot in front of Mr. Landen's Library. The building looked like all the other shopping centers in the little middle-of-nowhere town. Still, Charles sprang toward it with a happy gait. This was his big chance. When the lawyer had explained the inheritance from his uncle, Charles couldn't believe his lucky stars.

He had bankrupted four business ventures, including the shoe store his father had left him. He didn't have the knack for sales. Actually, Charles admitted to being pretty much useless. But this, this he knew he could keep going. The foundation trust with investments in mutual funds provided a sweet income and the funds for new purchases when necessary. The membership, though small, covered the overhead costs neatly. He could live comfortably for the rest of his life; being that he was but 28, it would be a long and happy one.

The scent of wood and aged paper greeted him as Charles inspected his latest inheritance. Looking about, he was astounded at the quaint charm the place exuded, as if he had been transported to an earlier age. In the front sections were modern books, even tables highlighting new best sellers, organized on intricately carved built-ins. Quiet nooks with power outlets gave patrons cozy spots for reading and working. The small kitchenette, located near the door marked 'office' was well-stocked with two Keurigs and a wide variety of coffees as well as cookies, trail mixes, and other snacks. The stainless steel refrigerator held water and sodas galore.

"I'll have to hire an assistant to manage all this and the bookkeeping," Charles mumbled as he made his way toward the back. A man had to know his limitations and he was determined not to fail this time. He would need help.

Surprised, Charles noted that, thus far, there appeared to be no damage of any kind. The lawyer had said his uncle was burned alive inside the special collection room of the library. He had expressed concern at the status of this prime asset.

Opening the door to the back room, Charles gasped. Standing in the threshold the new business owner marveled at the sight. A small circle of the expensive Persian rug and two sofa chairs were charred to a crisp along with what had clearly been an end table.

That was all.

Nothing else had been touched by the fire. Nor was there any water damage as the lawyer had suggested there could be from the sprinklers. The leather-bound books with gold and silver lettering rested safe and sound nestled into the great oak and mahogany bookcases. The room was a lot bigger once inside than he would have thought from the outside. There were several other reading areas interspersed between the aisles.

Standing in the center, Charles' voice echoed cheerily "Hello library! I'm your new owner and we are gonna live long and prosper!" He chuckled at his good fortune.

"Welcome!" The word, a whisper, swayed through the building and brought a chill down Charles' spine. Looking wildly around, he ascertain that he was indeed alone.

"Nah." Shaking his head in disbelief, Charles headed to the door marked office.

 Subscribe to Inklings Publishing's newsletter for information on new releases and upcoming events.
http://mrlandenlibrary.blogspot.com/

# Other Books by
# Inklings Publishing &
# Inklings Children Division

Enjoy more short stories in the Eclectic Writings Series anthologies. Featuring a variety of great authors and each based on a theme, this collection will surprise and entertain. Get your copy of each of the four volumes in the series today!

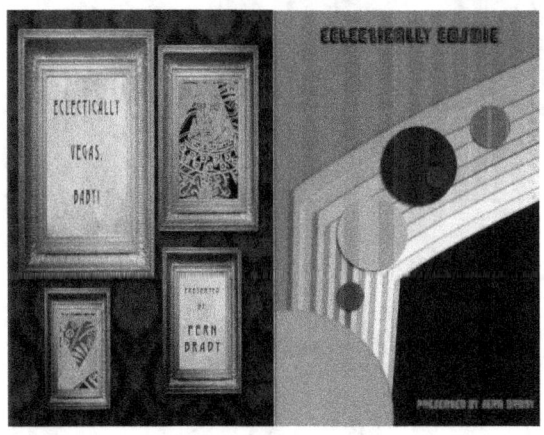

The Twisted Reveries series by Meg Hafdahl debuted in October 2015 with *Thirteen Tales of the Macabre*. In October 2016, *Tales from Willoughby* followed. Get your copy of these spine-tingling volumes today, and enjoy short stories by this great new female voice in horror!

Discover *Blood on the Potomac*, a spy romance from Melissa Algood. Follow Samantha Locke and Matthew Hale as she seeks her father's killer and he seeks his friend's. Together, they will fight to learn the truth.

This international legal thriller is the first book in the Roberto Duran series. Get to know this intrepid criminal attorney from Houston as he fights to uncover the truth and save a young Mexican socialite from wrongful incarceration.

This bilingual resource will provide insight into the workings of a civil lawsuit in terms anyone can understand. Great for interpreters, as well as authors who are writing legal thrillers.

Interpreters'
Anatomy *of a*
Civil Lawsuit

Anatomía *de un*
Juicio Civil *para*
Intérpretes Judiciales

Ramón M. del Villar

Attorney at Law
Federally Certified Court Interpreter
State Licensed Court Interpreter

Licenciado en Derecho
Intérprete Judicial Certificación Federal
Intérprete Judicial Texas, Maestría

Love, faith, politics, and longing expressed in beautifully crafted verse are waiting for you in this great compilation of Spanish poetry by Rio Grande Valley poet, Flavio Hinojosa, Jr. Delve into the power of poetic emotion expertly crafted to explore the different aspects of life!

El Globipelotón Risueño
Smiley Face Blatoon
by Lady Nefari Ydarb
Illustrated by Araceli Casas

*The Smiley Face Blatoon*, now available in a bilingual Spanish/English edition, launched Inklings Children Division in Summer 2015. Winner of the Texas Authors Association's First Place for Best Picture Book for all Ages, this, and all Inklings Children books, contains extensive activities, discussion questions, and cross-curricular work, as well as other tools for parents and educators.

Perceptions Series
Volume One

Edited by: Fern Brady

The Perceptions Series anthologies are a collection of short stories, poems, and nonfiction articles based on themes written for children grades three through six by a variety of authors. As with all Inklings Children Division books, each volume contains questions and activities for parents and educators to extend learning.

**Follow Inklings Publishing by:**

 Signing up for our newsletter on our website www.inklingspublishing.com

 Liking our Facebook page

 And following our tweets